Tangled Threads

A Hmong Girl's Story

Pegi Deitz Shea

CLARION BOOKS * NEW YORK

The characters and events in this book are fictitious. Any similarity to real persons, living or dead, is coincidental and not intended by the author. While the locations in Thailand and Providence are actual, events have been fictionalized for dramatic purposes.

Clarion Books
a Houghton Mifflin Company imprint
215 Park Avenue South, New York, NY 10003
Copyright © 2003 by Pegi Deitz Shea

The text was set in 13-point Bembo.

www.houghtonmifflinbooks.com

Printed in the U.S.A.

Library of Congress Cataloging-in-Publication Data
Shea, Pegi Deitz.
Tangled threads : a Hmong girl's story / by Pegi Deitz Shea.
p. cm.
Summary: After ten years in a refugee camp in Thailand, thirteen-year-old Mai Yang travels to Providence, Rhode Island, where her Americanized cousins introduce her to pizza, shopping, and beer, while her grandmother and new friends keep her connected to her Hmong heritage.
ISBN 0-618-24748-3
[1. Refugees—Fiction. 2. Hmong (Asian people)—Fiction. 3. Hmong Americans—Fiction. 4. Grandmothers—Fiction. 5. Embroidery, Hmong—Fiction. 6. Orphans—Fiction. 7. Providence (R.I.)—Fiction.] I. Title.
PZ7.S53755Tan 2003
[Fic]—dc21   2003002362

MP 10 9 8 7 6 5 4 3 2

FOR NANA (VINCENA KENNEDY DEITZ)

Chapter 1

I was nearly thirteen when the stomach fever exploded. The sick spells had been coming more frequently, each worse than the one before. Grandma never took me to the American or European doctors volunteering in the refugee camp. Only the shaman could rid my body of its bad spirits. Only the shaman could unite my wayward souls.

As always, Grandma knelt alongside me as I thrashed on the floor of our tiny hut. I could make no sense of what was inside me and what was out. The shaman was shaking his rattle and chanting for Saub to come to my side. His finger bells clinked. Or was it the ring of bomb shrapnel against stone? Was that his gong or the drumming of bullets into tree trunks? Or the *tup tup tup* of bullets sinking into skin? The shaman's incense made my stomach lurch. Everything—the heat, the noise, the putrid smells, the hot, sour vomit in my mouth—made my stomach lurch.

Even though we were safe in Thailand, the sickness always brought with it the sounds from the war in Laos.

Mother and father voices, screams, orders, the wails of babies. My own cries. But my grandmother's cry was different this time. Her hand slid back and forth over my sweaty forehead as she chanted, "It is time, Mai." Her voice, cool as rain running off a palm leaf, poured into my ear. Yes, time to die. Time to stop the pain.

The next thing I felt was warm threads of morning sun, weaving through the bamboo walls of our hut. I was alive. And my gut still ached. Then I felt the white cotton strings, seven of them, tied around my wrists to bind my life souls. The shaman and the others had done *khi tes* seven times? The shaman must have learned I was really sick! The only time I'd ever seen so many strings was the year before, when Grandma's friend had died. I wasn't afraid to die anymore. The Ancestral Kingdom had to be better than this refugee camp.

I found Grandma outside our hut. Hunched over our small burner, she was steaming rice for our breakfast.

"How do you feel?" she asked.

"Hungry as a boar," I replied. When had I eaten last?

Grandma gave me a heaping bowl. "You'll need your strength for such a big day."

As I chewed, I wondered what could make a day big in Ban Vinai. A new shipment of hand-me-down clothes from the Red Cross? I badly needed a bigger blouse or two. Could it mean a rare delivery of fish, or new schoolbooks from Bangkok? I swallowed and raised my eyebrows at Grandma.

"This morning, soon, Yang Cher will take us for interviews," she said.

"What?" I cried, jumping up.

"The camps will close next year, so we must go to interviews now or be sent back to Laos."

Interviews meant only one thing: We finally might go to America! We could live with my uncle and cousins, who had left the camp five years ago! I could not believe our good luck. I never understood how refugees were chosen to leave. We just had to wait until the workers called our names, Grandma had always told me. It frustrated me that I could do nothing to *make* them call us. But now they had!

Oh, I had to get ready. I dug through my basket to find the cleanest blouse and sarong wrap. I finger-combed my long brown hair, still matted from the fever. I twisted it into a neat bun above my forehead. Then I untied the pile of faded letters from my cousins, See and Pa Cua, and studied some of their American words. "Hello, I am Mai Yang," I practiced, putting my clan name last, like people do in America. "I like Coke!" See and Pa Cua. And Uncle Ger and Aunt Pa Khu. I might be with all of them soon!

Later that morning I easily spotted Yang Cher walking toward our hut. He was taller and thinner than most Hmong men, and he had to duck under the eaves of the thatched roofs in the alleys. Though he didn't smile or talk much, everyone liked him and trusted him like a brother. He had helped hundreds of

Hmong go through the confusing process of leaving.

We set off, picking our way between huts. The camp was a maze of crowded paths, following no straight line. Hmong had helped build the camp way back before I was born. It was meant to hold 10,000 people—not to pen in the 40,000 who lived here now. The Thai had built other camps too, and I bet they were just as crowded and miserable. Nobody knew the Communists would force so many of us Hmong from our villages. Nobody knew we'd have no place to go.

The paths among the huts were like the jungle paths we had taken to the Mekong River to escape Laos. Those curved around thick trees, veered to the narrowest part of a stagnant stream to cross, and doubled back up hills, away from the enemy. Here in Ban Vinai we stepped around mothers nursing their infants and children squatting to pee. I had become used to the stench. But that day I held my nose and tried not to get anything on me. The grownups used the latrines, but kids just squatted and pooped in the alleys. I never did! Well, once when the sickness came upon me suddenly. Oh, I couldn't wait to try the American indoor toilets, which my cousins had described but I still could not imagine.

We hurried onto the rutted main road through Ban Vinai. Grandma opened a black umbrella to shield herself from the sun. Hmong refugees, Thai soldiers, and Western round-eyed workers bustled about in the usual morning rush. I envied the women who got paid to cook in the restaurant for the pale-skinned workers. Mmm—I could have grown fat on the fried-pork aroma alone! All we got was rice. Dried fish if we were lucky.

Along the road, in little stalls, blacksmiths fired up their forges to make knives and tools. Old women spread mats on the ground to sell bunches of cilantro and chilies. Some Hmong who had rich relatives in America, or who had jobs in camp, scooted by on minibikes. They acted terribly important. When Uncle Ger lived here, he had a regular bicycle. He used to give See, Pa Cua, and me rides on the seat or the handlebars. Once he fit all of us on his bike. The tires flattened out, and we couldn't stop wobbling and giggling.

Soon we came up to the Widows' Store, where Grandma and I did needlework. As usual, the girls and women had displayed their *pa'ndau*—storycloths and patterns—for sale to the camp workers and the traders from Chiang Khan and other Thai cities. They were sorting their threads and materials for the new day of sewing, exactly as I had done since I was seven, when my cousins left for America. Grandma and her grandma and her ancestors had done the same for thousands of years. And now we would do it for another thousand years in America.

I hollered to my best friend. "Pa Nhia, guess what! I'm all better, and now we're going to talk to the Americans!"

Pa Nhia's face stretched wide in a smile. She knew

5

how much this meant to me. "Do you have enough food?" she asked. "Remember, it took us all day." I nodded, and she called, "Good luck!"

Luck? Why would I need luck? And why did all the women look so surprised? At once they began whispering to one another. Maybe they were jealous. I wouldn't blame them, I thought. I had burned with envy whenever I saw Hmong leave Ban Vinai—Hmong who hadn't spent ten years in the camp, as we had. I wasn't mad at Pa Nhia, though. She had come to the camp around the same time I did, and she would leave next month. But her uncle had decided the family would return to Laos. Poor Pa Nhia!

I started to ask Grandma why the women were gossiping, but she had already turned away from her friends. I was so ecstatic, I simply shrugged and ran to catch up to her. Usually Grandma was the slow one, but today the sickness had left me weak.

The office was one of the only camp buildings with solid walls and a complete roof. I'd never set foot in any of them. Inside, I'd been told, there were lots of telephones and typewriters—machines I had only heard of. Now I would see for myself. Maybe I could even touch one.

Outside the office Yang Cher sat us on the ground in a line with other refugees. Watching him enter the building, I felt proud that he was representing us. He had been Grandma's village leader back in Laos, and he had fought alongside the Americans during the war there and in Vietnam. He could have gone to America years ago, but he had stayed in camp to help people. He translated between the round-eyed camp workers and the Hmong refugees. He even trained teachers to spread the new Hmong alphabet to both boys *and* girls. I had learned to read and write Hmong, and I knew a little English. I practiced my *nitnoy Thai,* my few words of the local language, every month when the *pa'ndau* traders came from Chiang Khan to buy our cloths and bring us new supplies.

Grandma pulled out cross-stitch work and handed some to me.

"I can't sew," I said, waving it away. "I'm too excited."

Grandma's fingers flew across the blue material, leaving bright gold lines. I took a green silk thread as long as my arm and wound it around my finger. I let my fingertip get as purple as an orchid bud before unwinding it.

I didn't recognize anybody in line with us. Mostly women and children. And there, a handsome boy maybe five years older than me, with a toddler about two years old. A little brother?

I felt ashamed I knew so few others who lived only a few minutes' walk from my hut. But how could I know all 40,000 people in this camp?

People came and went all the time. They all came from Laos, but they went in many directions—France, Australia, Guyana, or America. After my cousins left, all I had was Pa Nhia and Grandma. I was friendly with the ladies and girls who stitched *pa'ndau* with me at the

Widows' Store. And I knew a few kids from reading class. But the faces in the long food and water lines were a blur of crying babies and stooped mothers.

I longed for the faces of my cousins. I kept their pictures in a special *pa'ndau* bag I had made. They looked so American in their indigo jeans. Some of the Western workers here wore such pants.

Out of the corner of my eye I caught Yang Cher walking toward us. He motioned for us to come. I helped Grandma off the ground, and we hurried behind Yang Cher into a large room with long tables. Under the tables, wires curled like magical snakes and stretched to the walls. Women as well as men spoke into telephones and worked the typewriters sitting on the tables. I wanted badly to touch one. I wanted to make it go *tappa tappa tappa* and have words appear on paper.

We sat in front of a young lady with skin as pale as coconut milk. Yang Cher translated her questions to Grandma: How do you spell your name? Where were you born? What boring questions, I thought. I couldn't help letting my eyes wander over the refugees sitting at desks with white ladies or men. Some faces showed worry, confusion, and pain. The teen boy—his eyes wide with hope. The baby, clapping, so happy. Oh, let *us* leave happy, I begged silently. Yet when I turned back to our interview, I didn't see any happy faces. Pa Nhia's wish for luck still rang in my ears.

Yang Cher's nostrils flared as he whispered harshly to Grandma, "You had a duty to do what was best for her."

Grandma cast her eyes down and muttered, "I did my duty."

"What? Grandma, is everything all right?" I asked.

Grandma nodded. "Everything is fine."

I took a deep breath and looked at the interviewer. The lady showed no anger. In fact, she was tilting her head slightly and speaking softly to Yang Cher.

To my surprise, when she finished, they both faced *me*. Yang Cher said, "The American asks if you want to leave Ban Vinai."

I dug my fingernails into my knuckles to make myself stop trembling. I stared out the window behind the lady and replied in Hmong, "More than anything." I must have said the right thing, because the lady grinned as she stamped our papers. The thuds sounded hopeful to me, like distant thunder after a dry spell. She bounced the papers this way and that way to make a neat pile. Then she handed them over to Yang Cher.

Interview upon interview blurred the rest of the day. The agency names were just clusters of letters that didn't spell anything. CRS. LBA. Yang Cher explained them to us, but I didn't understand everything. The officials were wearing colorful short-sleeved shirts, but some of them spoke sternly, like the uniformed soldiers. This lady was the EAO—Ethnic Affairs Officer. She was the nicest. JVA—Joint Voluntary Agency—was another agency. UNHCR—United Nations High Commissioner for Refugees. INS—Immigration and Naturalization Service. They asked so many questions, the same questions, over and over, that I wanted to scream, "Just let us go!"

The meanest person was the Immigration man. And he was ugly too. I could see his fat belly between the buttons of his shirt. He told Grandma to raise her right hand and testify about my father's military career.

"He repaired planes at Long Chieng," she said. "He fought for General Vang Pao and the American CIA."

"How did he die?" the officer asked.

Grandma stuck her chin out and said, "He was home visiting his wife when yellow rain fell upon their village."

The officer rolled his eyes, stopped writing, and waved his hand. English, Lao, and Hmong words flew faster and louder among Grandma, the officer, and Yang Cher. I couldn't pick out many words together, and hearing the tones was impossible when they all spoke at once. But I knew what they were arguing about. The Thai, the Lao, even most Americans didn't believe that the Pathet Lao—the Communists who were the new rulers of Laos—had used poison gas against us after the Vietnam War. But the Hmong knew. Grandma said the poison dotted the green husks of our corn. It strangled my parents and other villagers. It made babies be born without legs and arms.

We stitched these horrors into our *pa'ndau*. No one would ever forget, we vowed. The world would know.

But now, here, would Grandma's anger make the officer say, "No, they can't go" or "Send them back to

Laos"? Oh, Grandma, please, please be quiet, I silently begged.

At last the officer sighed and held his palms up to stop the argument. "How, then," he said very slow, very flat, "did the grandmother and the only child escape?"

I felt choked. Sometimes life without my parents made me wish I'd died with them. Then we could have entered the Ancestral Kingdom together. I couldn't bear to hear about their death again. I covered my ears, but it didn't help.

Grandma began the familiar story. "My son had come home from the fighting. He and his wife wanted time alone, so I took the toddler away into the jungle for a few hours to gather coconuts and roots. I heard the planes come, and we took shelter in a cave. With my own eyes I saw them drop the yellow rain."

Grandma's voice shook. "Much, much later we went back. Those who weren't vomiting, bleeding, or running crazy with fever were dead. My son and his wife were dead, bleeding from their noses and mouths and ears. . . . Excuse me." Grandma paused and wiped her tears in the crook of her sleeve. "They were never buried properly. Their souls were never released. Who knows where their souls are wandering now?"

I had to hide my own tears. I fumbled with Grandma's sewing bag and pulled out my favorite storycloth, my first storycloth. I ran my fingers over the threads I'd sewn years ago. The coarse stitches of my strong father, the smooth ones of my gentle mother, the wavy ones of the Mekong River, the white stitches of the plane that I dreamed would carry us to America. Someday.

"Help me be strong," I whispered to my parents' spirits. To my stitched cousins, I added, "Reach out and bring me to you!"

Grandma finished her story. "Mai lay down between her parents awhile. But then I heard gunfire. I took the baby and ran in the direction my other son had shown me, a week before. We ran for days and days to reach the river. He and his family ended up here. We did too. They left for America five years ago, and now we want to go."

"Why *now?*" Yang Cher translated.

My mind filled with pictures sent by my cousins: the two of them playing in curling salt water in Rhode Island, building a man with the thing they called snow, and reading big colorful books. I wanted to shout to the officer: "We want to be with what's left of our family." But to speak out, to speak instead of Grandma, would have been disrespectful.

Grandma finally whispered, "For Mai's health. For more powerful shaman."

My health? What about our family? Wasn't that most important? Perhaps Yang Cher had told her that "family" wasn't enough of a reason for the round-eyed officers to give our papers the stamp of approval. After Yang Cher offered a short explanation, the officer stamped them.

Yang Cher's shoulders relaxed. "It is settled. You can leave soon. I'll let you know a few days ahead of time."

Grandma, perhaps tired, lowered her head and shook it.

My eyes squeezed tight and I thanked the great Saub, and also Pa Nhia for her luck.

Chapter 2

April. Hot season. The weeks dragged on like a high simmer kept from a boil. Grandma and I ate, did chores, and sewed. Although Grandma was never one to chatter, she seemed especially quiet. How could anything be wrong, now that we were leaving this disgusting camp? I didn't dare question her. She might become angry and refuse to leave.

Pa Nhia and I couldn't stop dreaming about our new lives. We often sat by the barbed-wire fence and looked out into the jungle. "I hear there is no land in America—just skyscrapers and highways," Pa Nhia said one afternoon.

"I don't care," I said. "I will jump over every skyscraper and drive a car—real fast—on the highways."

Pa Nhia poked me with a stick. "*Ruam!* You've never been in a car, and now you're driving on a highway."

"Yes! And you'll still ride on a cart pulled by a skinny old water buffalo."

Pa Nhia didn't laugh. Aimlessly, she drew in the dirt between her feet with a stick.

I felt horrible. I hated the Pathet Lao who killed my parents and I would never return to Laos. But Pa Nhia was looking forward to being free anywhere. "I'm sorry," I said. "That was a mean thing I said about the cart. You'll have lots of things—your family all together again, the beautiful mountains all around you, animals, land to farm . . ."

Pa Nhia's chin lifted. "I can't wait to grow things— food, all kinds of food. Tangles of peas, knobs of ginger, and flowers! I will drape chains of jasmine around my neck."

Pa Nhia and I continued to stitch each day at the front of the Widows' Store. The older women stayed in the shady back. Happily, I sold three *pa'ndau* to the traders from Chiang Khan. Now I'd have some money for our trip if the lucky day ever came.

The day did come for Pa Nhia and what was left of her family. I walked with her to the buses. Usually she did most of the talking when we were together, but she barely spoke to me now. Wordlessly, we exchanged *pa'ndau* gifts. She gave me a stuffed turtle with a heart on its shell. I gave her an elephant with its trunk up, for luck.

"You said you would have an address for me—to write to," I reminded her.

As she fumbled with the piece of paper, she started to cry. "At first I was so happy that we would leave Ban Vinai, I didn't care where we went. But now I'm afraid the Lao soldiers will do things to the girls, to me . . . like the Thai soldiers did here."

15

I could feel my own tears gathering. I hugged her so I could tell her good things while she couldn't see my eyes. "No . . . things are different now, better. The fighting has stopped and there will be many more Westerners helping the Hmong too, building huts and water wells. Yang Cher told us himself. And, Pa Nhia, no one will hurt you."

"Please write," she pleaded. "I'll never forget you."

Her uncle gently pulled her onto the crowded bus. I stayed, waving, while it rolled out. The dust mixed with my tears and burned my eyes like chili paste.

A few weeks later, Yang Cher came to our hut and announced we'd be leaving in two days. I wrote a short letter to Pa Nhia, giving her our new address in Rhode Island.

Maybe someday you can visit us and stay in America awhile. I hear the houses are huge.

Until then I will hold our memories in my heart. I will never forget our secret spot by the camp border, where the water drained out into the jungle. Why did your boats always beat mine? And please, Pa Nhia, never let go of the pa'ndau elephant I made for you. It will bring you luck. I'll make you a new animal when I get to America, an American animal.

I hope that everything is going well in Laos and that your family is happy and that the rumors of bad land and harsh soldiers aren't true. I can't wait to read your voice in my first American letter. Write soon!

Our last night in camp Grandma banged the pots and utensils around but didn't say a word. I ran into the moonlight so her grouchy mood wouldn't darken mine, high as the moon itself.

Squatting in front of our hut, I brushed dirt off the golden glass mosaic I'd made years ago. It had taken me and my cousins weeks of digging through the garbage bins behind the workers' cafe to find enough Singha beer bottles. Then I had sunk them, neck first, into our patch of dirt. My pattern made an eight-pointed star. I had thought the Hmong star would protect us and bring us luck. We hadn't had much luck until recently, but I guess the star had protected us. Some refugees were beaten and raped by Thai soldiers, like Pa Nhia had been. Nothing like that had happened to Grandma or me.

The next morning I couldn't contain my joy. I ran to the bus taking us to the transition camp at Phanat Nikhom—a twelve-hour ride. Grandma walked slowly behind me.

"Come on, Grandma!" I stopped for the third time to wait for her. "We might miss the bus."

"Hush! My eyes are saying goodbye."

I shook my head. How could anybody feel sad to leave such a horrible place? I had only a few memories of my village life before we fled Laos—walking among pecking chickens, riding on my mother's back to the cornfields, tapping bamboo to make music. But how— even after ten years—could anyone consider this filthy camp home?

When we reached the bus, refugees were already leaning out of the windows the way they had when Pa Nhia left. They pressed hands one last time with loved ones, everyone wailing. How often had I been left behind! Now it was *my* turn to go. I was grateful to be leaving no one behind.

Grandma shoved her bag in front of her and stumbled up the steps of the bus. "It's too full," she complained. "Maybe we should go next time."

What I did next was very disrespectful. I was so afraid Grandma would turn around that I leaned against her backside and pushed! Luckily, no one saw this rudeness to an elder. A man might have scolded me or slapped me.

As I tried to follow Grandma into the aisle, I understood her complaint. The high-pitched voices deafened me. All I could see were faces, arms and legs, plastic sacks, cloth bundles. But no seats.

"Move on back," the driver ordered in Thai. "We have fifteen more to fit in."

Grandma and I picked our way over toddlers playing in the aisle and bundles containing the twenty-four hours' worth of cooked rice and water each family had been told to pack. We passed the handsome boy and the little one I'd seen together in the office. They'd made it too! I tried not to stare. I didn't know why it was so hard to take my eyes away from them.

Grandma found empty seats two rows behind the boy and two rows from the back. The floor curved up in front of the window seat—it must have been where the wheel was located. I had seen those curves on the small open trucks that delivered goods to the camp. I squeezed into the space and Grandma sat beside me. As soon as we'd settled, a mother plopped a whining child next to Grandma and sat across the aisle with her other two children.

Soon the motor rumbled, and gravel kicked against the floor under me and made my feet tickle. My first ride in a bus, in any motor vehicle! I pressed my nose to the window. I kept waiting for someone to come on board and say, "Yang Mai, off! There's been a mistake!" Or perhaps the bus would break down, or the gate would get stuck. I feared that I was dreaming all this good luck. But no. The gates of the camp swung open.

"Oh!" I heard myself gasp. Outside for the first time in ten years!

The bus quickly picked up speed. I stood and stuck my arm out the window. The wind lifted my hand as if it were a wing. But squirms and squeals soon broke the spell. The child next to Grandma was vomiting. I snatched our food and pa'ndau off the floor just in time. I covered my nose and mouth when I heard, saw, smelled others retching because of the crowded, bumpy ride.

"It's going to be a long trip," Grandma muttered.

Spotting a yellow puddle under a child in the aisle, I agreed.

"Hmong," she said, "are not meant to desert their homelands."

"Thailand is not Laos," I stated.

"The mountains are our homelands. This is the same."

Those words alarmed me. The land outside Ban Vinai *was* beautiful. Towering mountains, steep valleys, bright flowers and waterfalls. Sometimes the cliffs dropped off so sharply, I couldn't see the road beneath us. The sights made me dizzy with glee. I'd never seen so many different greens in my life. But I reminded myself that we were leaving it for a better place now. And I knew America must be the prettiest place of all.

Soon Grandma pulled out some *pa'ndau,* reverse appliqué, her specialty. When she applied a shape to another piece of cloth, it looked like it was one smooth piece. She neatly, quickly tucked under all the edges of the shape and sealed them with hidden stitches.

"What are you working on?" I asked.

"Diamond-in-the-square."

Grandma wasn't taking any chances! The diamond-in-the-square stood for the altar Hmong kept in their homes. Was this her way of bringing our ancestors with us?

I took out my stitchwork—a pattern of cucumber seeds to make our new life fruitful. But even a simple chain stitch was impossible. The sharp turns and sudden bumps made my needle jump like a flea. Putting the cloth down, I admired Grandma's steady fingers.

"This," Grandma said, smoothing out the *pa'ndau,* "is what made your grandfather marry me. And what made my son marry your mother."

"Really?" I pictured my father and mother tossing the

ball in the courting ritual at New Year. My mother's *pa'ndau*-decorated costumes must have shone above the other women's. Perhaps she'd stitched a long black dress blooming with pink and green flowers. Did she tuck all her hair up under her black-banded hat? Was the jingly music of her silver collar sweeter than anyone else's?

Grandma repeated the age-old truth: "The better a Hmong woman can work, the better the wife she'll make."

Even though I had a special gift for needlework, I couldn't picture any boy tossing a ball with me. I was too scrawny. Too weak from sickness. Hmong men liked sturdy women who could have lots of babies. Women who could work all day in the fields and cook delicious food at night.

After a long while the mountain roads gave way to a two-lane highway running between flat plains. Homes on stilts reminded me of old hens on skinny legs. Children rode on the backs of swaying water buffalo. Green shoots of rice peeked up from flooded paddies. It amazed me to see people just walking or driving or pedaling anywhere they wanted. I wanted to ask everyone, "Where are you going?"

Shortly, the bus stopped. Red-and-white shop signs blinked by the roadside. Yellow awnings shaded people sipping drinks at outside tables. Stalls displayed fruits and vegetables like offerings to ancestors. Green *tuk tuk* carts motored in all directions with their passengers.

"We need gas," the driver barked. His sunglasses

showed in the wide mirror over his head. "You may get off to use the bathroom."

I couldn't wait to stretch my legs, and to smell something other than urine, vomit, and bus exhaust. I helped Grandma squat at the drain in the ladies' room. After I relieved myself, I wandered outside. All the refugees were filing back on the bus obediently. I didn't want to return to the bus until I had to. Grandma hadn't come out yet. I had time.

Bursts of color drew me away from the bus. Fresh fruit! When I reached the stand, I ran my fingers over the fuzz of a red rambutan, the hardness of a purple mangosteen, the waxy flesh of a yellow jackfruit. I hadn't tasted any of these since New Year in December, seven months ago. And now all of the fruits were begging me to take them along, to eat them. I wanted all of them, but I wanted my money too. Still, could I spare a few coins for a sweet, chewy rambutan?

I asked the vendor the price in Thai: *"Tao ri?"*

The man eyed the bulging bus and asked, *"Meo?"*

My face immediately tightened at the insult. Who was he to call Hmong "barbarians"?

The vendor grinned widely, showing dark-red betel-stained teeth. He moved to the far stand and threw out his hands. "These from America. Called *apple.*"

I recognized the word "America." I drifted over to the display and touched the shining round fruit. "Ah pul," I tried. *"Tao ri?"*

"Sip baht," the vendor said, still smiling.

Ten *baht?* That was the price of a whole meal at the camp restaurant! *"Paang mahk!"* I tried to negotiate to half the price. *"Ha baht."*

But the vendor shook his head and smacked his lips. *"Alloy mahk!"* He cupped an apple in his hands as if it were the last sip of water on earth. *"Baat baht."*

"Come, Mai!" Grandma called out the bus window. "We're leaving!"

The bus coughed and spat stinky smoke. I dug a small *pa'ndau* purse from my bag and pulled out eight *baht.* The bad man transferred the apple to my hands. Rubbing it clean on my blouse, I ran to the bus.

The driver yelled at me as I boarded. "Next time you use the bathroom only. That's all!" He lurched the bus forward, and I fell down in the aisle. Holding my prized apple in the air, I landed on a pile of giggling toddlers. Someone helped me up. The guy with the little boy! How kind. I lowered my eyes and thanked him.

I climbed across Grandma, then offered her the first bite. "It's from America. Want a taste?"

Grandma nodded, her eyes twinkling for the first time. "You first."

I took a deep breath, then bit the tight red skin. Tartness and sweetness squirted back to where my jaw met my ears. After I handed Grandma the apple, I wiped my hand across my mouth. Then I licked the juice from my fingers.

Grandma turned the apple around and bit. Her face screwed up at once. She parted her lips and pulled out a small green worm. I laughed very loud. The worm started wriggling in Grandma's pinch.

Grandma growled, "How much did you pay for this?"

"The worm was free!" I said.

Grandma was not amused. She handed me the worm and apple. "The worm is an omen, Mai. A bad sign."

I bowed my head to cut off my giggles. A bad sign, how? We were always picking bugs out of our rice before we cooked it. Holding the stem, I twirled the apple. I saw no other worm holes, so I took another bite. Mmm. Then another, and another. Tangy juice ran down my throat, and I closed my eyes. The squiggling worm tickling my palm was a *good* sign! It came all the way from America. And it was alive!

I decided to give the worm its freedom too. But by our next stop it had died.

Chapter 3

Late that night we arrived at the Phanat Nikhom transition camp—endless squares of buildings with thick walls and metal roofs. No mountains in the distance. Metal poles instead of trees. Tall fences with barbed wire. I was too tired to be glad we'd reached the next step. The lights on the poles didn't do much to keep the darkness away. Or the mosquitoes.

A Thai soldier shoved us and yelled, "Quick, now, or you'll be stomped. Go, go, go, you pigs." The soldiers shooed us into a large space surrounded by cement shelters. Grandma and I sat, nervous, among groups of cranky children and parents. The boy and the toddler sat on the other side of Grandma. She tried to ignore the little one's whines. I was just about to change places with her when an officer in a crisp green uniform strode out before us. Another followed him, translating the officer's stern Thai into Hmong.

"You must obey all rules, or else. Each family will be assigned to a quad of four long houses. If you're alone, we'll fit you where there's room. Six families to a house. Four houses to a bathroom. You must take turns cleaning the bathroom. You are allowed to go outside your quad only for classes and rations. Lights out at eight P.M. No going out of your house after eight. You men, take turns guarding your house. We are not responsible for . . ."

Even though we were closer to America, to my cousins, my dreams, I felt imprisoned once again. I tried to cheer myself up. Hadn't everyone who left Ban Vinai and the other camps gotten processed through Phanat Nikhom, even my cousins five years ago? Grandma and I wouldn't be stuck here forever.

As the man talked and talked, my head began to nod. I hadn't realized I'd fallen asleep until I felt a sharp pain. The same soldier who had called us pigs was jabbing a baton into my back and motioning for us to stand. He led us, the guy and the toddler, and some others to House 4 in Quad 2. As he left, the soldier made a kissing sound at me and promised, "I'll be back."

Grandma and I clutched each other and turned our faces from him.

The boy was stringing a rope across the room we had been assigned to. As he draped a black blanket over the rope, he said, "My name is Lor Yia. My son is Koufing. The far corner will be more private for you. Safer, too."

Son? Oh. . . . Where's Koufing's mother, I wondered. Dead? Must be. There was no other explanation for a mother abandoning her child. Through a space between the blanket and the cement floor, I watched Yia lie down with Koufing. I closed my eyes and tried to remember sleeping with my parents. The picture was hard to hold, like a bird feather on a windy day.

The next day workers showed us where to get food and water rations, and how to clean the latrine troughs. They gathered us again, then separated us by age. The soldiers led the old ones away. I grabbed for Grandma to keep her with me, but she motioned to the Thai and Western ladies leading my group. "Go to school, go on, and learn everything. I'll see you at supper."

In a bright clean room with chairs and desks, the ladies tested us children for classes. Since I could read and write Hmong and a bit of Thai and English, I entered the intermediate level of PASS, the Preparation for American Secondary School program.

That night at dinner I asked, "Grandma, what will you learn in your class?"

Grandma put down her empty bowl and got up from her crouch. She scuffed over to her *pa'ndau* bag and pulled out the reverse-appliqué pattern she had been doing on the bus. "There is no class for me," she muttered. "The old ones can't learn anything, the soldiers told us. We'll care for the babies. I will watch Koufing while his father learns a job."

Oh, I realized. This is going to be even more boring for Grandma than Ban Vinai. At least there she had the Widows' Store.

"It is just as well they don't put me in a school,"

Grandma said. "I already know how to watch a little one. And do a lot of other things too."

I shook my head. "Don't worry, Grandma. I'll teach you everything I learn."

In PASS I felt delirious. My mind and heart were bursting with new thoughts and feelings and actions. The other thirty kids looked just as excited to learn. Our Thai teacher, Miss Sayapong, wore beautiful clothes—shirts with ruffles, shoes that made her walk on her tiptoes, skirts that were quite high—above the knee. And she knew *everything!* Every day she gave us new American words. Each new word was a gift, a toy to play with. We watched American TV shows. Big Bird taught me letters and numbers. I learned funny songs about "up" and "down," "under" and "over." In the afternoons we played American games like basketball and baseball. Oh, I wanted to become a champion in all games!

And every evening I kept my promise to Grandma and tried to teach her. "Say 'cloth,' say 'thread,' say 'water,' say 'rice.'" Grandma repeated the words, but she never remembered them. The new language was like a brilliant dye that did not soak into her cloth.

The only thing I didn't like about going to school was passing that mean kissy soldier every day. He called me things, words in Thai I'd never learned and never wanted to learn. Was this the way Pa Nhia had felt in camp? Like a small bird being hunted? But even the soldier couldn't take away my delight with every new thing. I learned to vacuum, to cook, to iron. To look out a peephole. I learned to sit on an American toilet without falling in! To make an American bed, one that had legs. Life in America would spill over with games, with a new word called "fun." After two months I graduated from PASS and received an award for language.

Yia came home full of hope too. "I can get a job fixing all kinds of machines. I can fix a car, but I have never driven one! Maybe you'll have something I can fix," he said to me.

Grandma came over and spoke before I could think of a clever reply. "My son, Mai's uncle, will be able to fix anything we need, I'm sure," she said, sitting between us.

She was doing that a lot, I realized. Grandma would not let Yia and me speak to each other alone. If Yia said something, she always answered before I could open my mouth. Or if Yia and I were cleaning together or playing with Koufing, she would sneak in between us. Grandma's behavior would have been normal if we were living in a village. Parents and grandparents always watched teenagers closely. But here in this camp we lived too close. How could we *not* talk? Whenever Yia and I found ourselves alone—for instance, when Koufing was napping—Grandma always crept up like a stalking tiger, the Tiger Mother who didn't want to share me.

One night when Yia had cleanup duty, I was bouncing Koufing on my knees and singing silly songs. He was giggling and squealing so much, I almost cried with joy. Koufing didn't know anything about war or killing. He probably couldn't remember his mother. None of that mattered right now. He had food and love, and that was all it took to make him happy.

Grandma's voice spoiled our fun. "Yia needs a mother for Koufing. You aren't ready to be a mother. And Yia has no money to offer for you. Besides, Yia is going to a place called Massachusetts. Your uncle Ger will find someone worthy of you in Providence."

How did she know what I felt and thought? Did she steal my dreams? Perhaps she was right, though. I couldn't picture myself as a mother running after children. And after that my dreams filled with skyscrapers, cars, and cool clear water. Providence.

The afternoon before our medical exam, I bathed myself and washed my hair. I dragged Grandma to the bathroom too. I wanted us to look perfect. I had heard that the doctors could keep unhealthy refugees back, or return them to camp. Even worse, to Laos! I didn't know what rumors to believe, but it was good to be prepared.

As we got ready for sleep that night, I asked Grandma. "What's the first thing you'll do in America?"

"I will grab Ger—my only child left after all that fighting—and make the years between us disappear."

I pictured myself, heads together with my cousins, telling silly secrets, doing *pa'ndau*, gobbling up the food they called pizza. "I'm . . . I'll . . ." All of a sudden water gathered in my mouth, and not from the thought of the magical food. I became dizzy, and my stomach pitched. My bowels cramped and rumbled.

"No!" I cried, and I raced for the latrines.

"Mai!" Grandma yelled. "The soldiers! The curfew!"

Retching into a floor drain, I soon felt Grandma's hand rubbing my back. I felt horrible—and even worse when Yia rushed in.

He asked, "Is everything okay?"

Wearily, Grandma explained, "Mai gets a fever in the stomach a lot."

"It can't be," I moaned. "I can't get sick now!"

"I'll get a wet cloth for her," Yia said, and he was gone. Good. How disgusting he must think I was. But he returned right away and said, "I'll wait out here in case a guard comes."

"Thank you," Grandma said, and she pressed the cool towel on the back of my neck. "Don't worry. The camp doctors can wait," she murmured. "We'll go for our examination another time."

How could she think "don't worry" and "another time"? I squatted in the trough, sweat popping from every pore, and sobbed, "There is no other time!"

And with this delirium the voices of the war returned, and unbearable pictures now too: Babies pounded in rice mills, women raped bent over like dogs, howling like dogs, blood—like rivers—evacuating spirits from the bodies poisoned by yellow rain. The war continued to rage inside me, keeping me from freedom, from my family in America.

Chapter 4

The first thing I was aware of, after, was peeling the salt-hardened hair from my face. I slowly rolled over to see refugees bustling about in the hot sun. I was in our house, but the blanket separating us from Yia and Koufing was gone. Their space was empty.

Grandma was sleeping beside me. I shook her and said, "Wake up, Grandma. The medical exam's today."

Grandma stirred and mumbled, "No, Mai. It wasn't meant to be."

"Please. What do you mean, 'wasn't meant to be'? And where are Yia and Koufing?"

Grandma remained curled toward the wall. "They have left for America. Our exam was two days ago, Mai. You slept through everything. Now *I* need to sleep."

Gone? Our only chance! "Grandma, please get up."

"Let me be, child," she mumbled, shooing my hands away. "I've been up with you day and night for three days. I need to rest."

I tore off a lavender thread from my sarong and wound it around my finger. I forced myself to calm down and think. I had to do something. Talk to somebody. Who would understand? And who would make the doctors understand?

A few minutes later I knocked on the door frame of the empty schoolroom. "Hello?" I called in English.

"Mai!" Miss Sayapong came to the door. "What a nice surprise to see you. I thought you'd be on your way to America already."

I didn't know how to translate my problem into English. So I spilled out in Hmong how we'd missed our medical appointment. Hopefully, I asked, "Can we get another soon?"

Miss Sayapong covered her mouth with her fingertips.

"Please, Teacher, help me," I pleaded. "I could die if I don't go to America soon. But we can't tell the doctors here that I'm ill, or else . . ."

I felt my legs give way. Miss Sayapong caught me and led me to a chair. She pressed my head down between my knees. After a few moments I pulled myself up.

"I'm okay now. It's only . . . I haven't eaten in a long time."

"Stay right here," Miss Sayapong said. "I'll get food." In a few minutes she returned with water, bananas, and sweet jasmine rice. "I just came up with a great idea. Leave everything to me, Mai."

Later, as the puddles from the afternoon rain evaporated, Grandma and I met Miss Sayapong at the medical clinic. Miss Sayapong led us inside, saying, "Let me talk. Don't say a word."

I couldn't keep up with the fast Thai spoken between

the woman at the desk and Miss Sayapong. But I could feel the nurse's skeptical eyes upon me. I lowered my gaze. Finally, after several impatient words, the nurse sighed and rustled a lot of paper. She showed the three of us into a room with a high table and slender instruments.

Impressed, I asked Miss Sayapong, "What did you tell the nurse?"

"I said you missed your appointment because you had gotten your first menstruation and were sick and frightened," Miss Sayapong whispered.

But that hadn't happened yet! "You told a lie?"

"Don't worry," she said, grabbing my hand. "Many, many horrible lies have put you here. Please allow me a tiny harmless lie to help get you out."

At once the rings on the curtain rod clanged together and a Thai man in a white coat appeared. "All clothes off, you two," he barked, closing the curtain behind him.

No one, except Grandma, had ever seen me with my clothes off! And I don't think I'd ever seen her undressed. We stood there, disbelieving our ears.

"I said, 'All clothes off,'" the doctor repeated, opening a file.

After Miss Sayapong nodded, we obeyed.

My eyes darted as I unbuttoned my shirt first. The doctor bowed his head and read a sheet of paper. Miss Sayapong began reading the posters on the walls. Grandma was busy unraveling her layers of black cloth, and I tried not to stare at her long breasts and folds of withered skin. Even though no one seemed to be watching *me*, I had never felt so small and helpless in all my life. I felt like the dried husk of a dead bug. *Oh, doctor, be blind to my body, to my sick, sick body.*

Miss Sayapong explained the tests to Grandma and me as the exam went on. They didn't hurt, really. But I gagged on the glass stick, bitter with rubbing alcohol. I feared the armband would squeeze my heartbeat away. That the pinching needle would suck all the spirits out of my blood. That the x-ray, the worst of all, would show my insides full of pus.

Everything was so different from Hmong medical practices. The doctor didn't chant like the shaman, and his magic didn't come from smoke and rattles and buffalo horns. The doctor called no souls home to the body. Was this doctor magical enough to see my sickness? And if so, was he magical enough to cure it and set me free?

The doctor pointed to Grandma and explained something in Thai. The only words I caught were "high" and "blood."

I tried to ask Miss Sayapong what was going on, but she waved away my concern. She told us Grandma's heart was not beating normally, but that was common from fear or old age and could be corrected in America. Still, the doctor couldn't tell us right away if we were healthy enough to leave Phanat Nikhom. "He ordered extra blood tests, and the results will take some time," Miss Sayapong said. "Plus the laboratory makes a delivery only once a week."

Time, time. I was so sick of time. How come I was the only one in a hurry? All the refugees had families waiting for them in America. Yet the mothers and grandmothers gossiped in the shade, as if the corn and rice had already been harvested and a roasted pig crackled on the fire. The children played volleyball and chased each other. The old men crouched and drew maps in the hard dirt and debated plans. And now that I had time, I missed the faces of Yia and Koufing. We'd been like a family, almost.

Six days after our medical exam we still hadn't heard from the doctor. Early the next morning I was walking in tiny steps across the quad, holding two full pails of water. A green form, blurry in the waves of heat, came toward me. A stack of papers flopped in his hand. Our medical exam results? Before I could take another step, the soldier stopped me. Oh, I knew those dark eyes even behind the black sunglasses. I knew his skinny lips. *Smooch, smooch,* they went. I hated that noise. I wanted to sew those lips together, sew his eyes shut! But if I did anything hurtful, the soldiers might send me to Laos and I'd never join my cousins.

"*Sawat di kop,*" he said, lifting my chin with his baton. "You go to America, Mai?"

His breath felt hot as dragon fire. How did he know my name? What else did he know? I didn't answer him.

"If you want to go to America, you have to come with me first," he said, rattling the papers.

From behind, he pushed me toward an office in the

Ministry of the Interior building. Water splashed as I stumbled along. Were there really more papers? Tests? What did he want with me?

The door swung open into an empty office. No desk, no papers.

"Stand right there and keep hold of the pails," he ordered. He shoved me forward, my face flattened to the wall. "I have to teach you what the American men do to little Hmong girls. If you scream, I will kill you. I will simply report that I caught you stealing."

The clinking of his belt buckle told me what he wanted to do to me. Pa Nhia's family would not let her talk about her rape. Too filthy. Too disgraceful. I hadn't wanted to hear it either, but I let her tell me. How the men came from behind like cowards, too shameful to show their faces. How animal. She said it was like being torn apart by a tiger from the inside out.

"Kill me," I begged him. "I'd rather die."

"Death is too good for you," he replied, clamping his right hand over my mouth.

His sweaty palm tasted rubbery from his baton. His other hand lifted the back of my sarong. I felt his hot bare skin against my backside, my arms useless at my sides.

My arms? The pails, the pails! I took a deep breath and dropped them on the soldier's feet.

"Ai!" he screamed, stumbling backward. The pails had drenched and tripped him.

I pushed past him, ran outside into the quad, and

bumped right into Miss Sayapong. I hid behind her as the soldier came out, wet from his knees down, zipping up his pants.

"Is there a problem?" Miss Sayapong asked him.

He spat on the ground and pointed at me. "Tell the *Meo* not to waste water rations again."

"Kop kum ka," Miss Sayapong said. I could hear anger behind the polite words.

After he left, she held me at arm's length to look me over. "Are you all right? He didn't . . . ?"

I couldn't speak. I just shook my head.

Miss Sayapong was silent for a moment. Then, holding up a paper, she cried, "Medical clearance! You and your grandmother can go next week."

I was still shaking. I had no idea what she was showing me. The Thai words were jumping all over the page.

"To America!" Miss Sayapong yelled.

"Oh!" I pressed my hands together in a *whai*. "How can I ever thank you for . . . for everything?"

Miss Sayapong placed her hands around mine and we touched foreheads. Then she said in English, "Keep learning, Mai. That is how to thank me."

"I will, Teacher," I said. "I'll never forget you."

Chapter 5

A week later our time to leave had finally come. Workers made all 150 of us line up and passed out cold-weather clothes. My body had never been cold. I couldn't wait to see what it felt like. Tables held long-sleeved blouses with stripes, swirly patterns, checks, dots; men's shirts that said "Chicago Bulls" and "Keep On Truck'n"; plaid slacks of the spongiest cloth. The children danced in their new outfits. The elders, used to dressing in blue and black, squatted, hiding their bright American clothes.

I put on a blue-striped shirt and a flowery yellow skirt and sneakers. "How do I look?"

Grandma shrugged. She wore a lime-green dress that had tiny furry balls on it. She squirmed in her new shoes. Her skin looked ashy.

We rode in a line of buses for about an hour. Then I spotted the buildings of Bangkok—tall ones in the middle, surrounded by wide flat ones. Alongside garbage-strewn canals were shacks as rickety as our huts in camp. But at least these people were free to go anywhere they wanted.

Just then a roar passed over our bus and rocked it. The adults moaned, the children cried. Right outside our window the belly of a huge plane floated by. I saw its wheels touch down ahead at the airport.

"Just think, Grandma," I said in awe. "We're going to ride in one of those beautiful things! And I thought cars and buses were special."

Stitching a snail-shell pattern, Grandma kept her head bowed. "I don't want to think about flying, Mai. I don't trust those iron hawks. Remember, I've seen them drop deadly things. And the planes don't always land on their feet."

The picture of such a plane crashing on its belly made me shiver.

A worker led us to the middle of the airport building and told us to wait. We all took off our shoes and sat on the floor. Oh, I saw hundreds of dressed-up people rushing in all directions, and I saw stores with beautiful things I had no words for. I swore, when I had American money, I'd buy everything!

The worker returned and hurried us toward the gate. Suddenly, he stopped and looked at my bare feet, then Grandma's, then everyone's. He slapped his forehead and said, "Dammit, I'll never learn." He took a few men and ran back into the terminal. They soon returned with all of our shoes, but they had no idea which shoes belonged to which people. *We* didn't even know which were ours. We hadn't had them for long. All the soft sneakers looked the same—swooshes and stripes. There were fancy dark shoes too, but all different sizes. I was too nervous and excited to care about shoes.

"We'll give them back on the plane," a Hmong leader decided. "We don't have time now."

Grandma grabbed my arm and said, "It is a sign! The shoes did not want to come. Our feet should not leave this land of our ancestors."

This land could keep the shoes! I'd buy American shoes. I giggled to think of arriving in America barefoot in the cold snow. Miss Sayapong had told us that American people didn't go anywhere without shoes. They weren't even allowed in stores without shoes! And they wore shoes in the house, too—the same ones that walked on the dirty street. Well, I didn't have to like *everything* about America.

Grandma kept muttering about signs and her precious mountains. I could understand that she didn't want to leave her ancestors. But the land itself? As the plane soared into the air, so did my heart. Goodbye, land of war, land of prisons, land of lies.

As on the bus, the refugees soon filled the plane with the stench of vomit. I thought it funny, actually. I got sick all the time on the ground, yet my body seemed to love moving on the clouds. To me the movement meant freedom. And the English words in a magazine in front of me seemed like a code, secret passwords to freedom. I hungrily searched for words I knew and tried to pronounce new ones: frequent flyer, duty-free liquor, oxygen. Of course, I didn't know what they meant. But I couldn't wait to learn.

After an hour or so the aroma of food made my stomach rumble. I kept looking behind me to count the number of rows until the food cart came to ours. Finally, a flight attendant set trays before Grandma and me. Gazing at all the colorful choices of foods, I didn't know where to start! Think of the food in PASS, I suggested to myself. Well, American cheese came in squares, so first I unwrapped a white square. It had a strangely sharp smell. I tasted a corner of the square and immediately pulled my tongue back from the bitterness.

"No, no, no, no, no," the attendant said, flapping like a fussy hen. She brought over a Hmong man, who translated. "You were not listening! She already explained to people: This is not for eating. This is for cleaning hands and face, for *after* you eat."

How embarrassing! How many Hmong had swallowed the folded white square? Maybe that's why everybody was vomiting. And what about cleaning hands *before* eating?

Grandma nodded at me and said, "You try everything, and if you like it, I will try it."

Drinking water from a bottle was probably safe. But what do I do with the clear squares in my cup, I wondered. I touched my tongue to one of them. It was so cold, my tongue stuck. I peeled the square thing off and threw it back in the cup.

Next, I unwrapped and smelled a round crusty ball. I

broke it in two, nibbled it, and recalled the taste at once.

"It's called 'bread,'" I told Grandma, "though we had only square bread in Miss Sayapong's class."

After we finished the bread, Grandma pointed to a brown mass in a little brown puddle on my tray. It looked like wood, but it smelled like the meat the workers ate in Ban Vinai. I took a bite, then gobbled it all down. Grandma ate hers, but she wasn't impressed. It did smell better than it tasted.

"Look, Grandma!" I pointed at my cup. "The squares changed into water." We shook our heads at each other. How were we supposed to know?

There were lots of small packets on our trays. Some had names I recognized from PASS. Grandma and I poured the sugar into our mouths and crunched the gritty stuff. Then I licked my fingertip and pressed it down on the salt. It tasted like the dried fish we had once in a while in Ban Vinai.

When Grandma tried a grain of the blacker pepper, she smiled and said, "It's hot, like chili."

A man across the aisle heard us. "Yes?" he exclaimed. "Like chili?" And he tipped the whole packet into his mouth. He coughed and gagged so much that he vomited onto his tray. The flight attendant had to pull down the mask above the man's head and give him oxygen! Another gave him a shot like the doctor had given me. Eating on a plane was dangerous!

After the trays were cleared, Grandma and I swayed down the narrow aisle toward the bathroom. The line stretched five people long—nothing compared to the lines of hundreds in camp. In the back a Hmong mother was showing her baby's messy bottom to a flight attendant. The attendant winced, pursed her lips, and backed away. She fumbled in a closet and came back with something she called a "diaper." No baby wore diapers in the mountain villages or camps, and anyway, how could plastic stop a mess? Then she pulled *me* to her, turned me, and taped the diaper in front of my skirt.

A Hmong leader translated, "The plastic goes on the outside. The cloth goes against the skin."

The smelly little toddler reminded me of Koufing. He pointed at me with the diaper hanging down and giggled. We all giggled, even the flight attendant. I untaped the diaper and stuck it on the wall.

Soon the bathroom door opened and Grandma took her turn. The door sprang closed behind her, yet opened again immediately. Grandma came outside, shaking her head. "How can you do it on a seat? Where does it go?"

"Don't worry," I said. "Look, you lift the top, then sit. It's like the one we had in our PASS class. A lot smaller, though."

Grandma kept shaking her head. "I won't sit on that hole. I'm so heavy, I'll fall through the sky. I'll wait."

"But we won't be landing in America for another six hours!"

"I can wait," Grandma replied.

I shook my head at Grandma's foolishness. But when

I pushed the button to flush, the loud whoosh of the toilet made me jump. Where *did* everything go? Into the ocean? People couldn't really fall through . . . could they? If I had to go again, I'd wait until we got to the airport too.

I must have napped awhile, because I awoke to the smell of more food. They should call airplanes air-restaurants, I thought. Grandma had already started to eat the bread. That was a good sign.

Land! The map in my magazine showed that the smile made of islands below belonged to America. "The Aleutians." Around them the water rippled and shone more brilliantly than the new metal roofing in the camp.

Seeing land after hours over the water, I grew excited again. A new school, new friends, my family all around me. I pulled out my old storycloth, my first one. Right beneath me were the curls of salt water—the Pacific Ocean. It wouldn't be long before I could touch the Atlantic Ocean and touch my cousins for real—cousins not made of silk thread on a *pa'ndau*.

Now we were flying at a lower level, and I could see better out the tiny window. In some places the shore fell off steeply into the ocean. In others the land eased into the lacy ribbon of surf, like a hemp skirt spread out to dry in the sun.

I felt restless, so I walked to the rear of the plane to stretch my legs. Two attendants were fixing their hair in front of a mirror. The attendant who'd explained about the diaper was named Nancy. She was pressing a pink stick over her lips. She smiled at me and said, "It's lip-stick. Want to try it?"

Oh, so that was how Miss Sayapong colored her lips some days! I'd never seen one before, and I did want to try. Nancy gave me a new tiny lipstick and held the mirror for me. I rubbed it on, then licked my lips. The attendants giggled when I wrinkled my nose at the waxy taste.

"Pretty!" Nancy said.

Was I really? I stood on tiptoe to see my reflection in their mirror. I looked a bit like Miss Sayapong, but without the greenish powder she wore on her eyelids and her dark curly lashes.

Nancy pinned golden wings on my blouse pocket and gave me the little lipstick to keep. "Thank you," I said in English.

Then I rushed back to Grandma. "Look! Pretty?" I asked, puckering my lips and sticking out my chest.

Grandma frowned. She dug in her *pa'ndau* bag and came out with an old cross-stitched piece. "Rub it off," she ordered.

My head started shaking no on its own. I'd never dis-obeyed Grandma before. Never.

"Out of false mouths come false words," she said. "Rub it off."

My head shook again, my eyes looking down.

"Then I will," she growled.

I squeezed my eyes shut as the rough cloth tore at my lips. I would not let her see my tears of pain. My mouth throbbed when she finished. My lips tasted as if they were holding steel sewing pins. I turned away from Grandma, stared out the window, and fingered my golden wings.

I hated her. Did I dare think that? I felt a strange thrill as I formed those words in my mind: I hated her. At that moment, with my lips throbbing, nothing else Grandma had done for me meant anything. Not the hours by my side tending my fevers, not the food she cooked each day, not the *pa'ndau* instruction, not the stories of my mother and father. She had hurt me. Deliberately. I hated her.

What did Grandma know about America? Nothing. Her own son could not even write to her, because she didn't know how to read. My cousins wrote me all about America. I was the one who studied America, who remembered every English word I ever learned. Grandma didn't know a thing about America.

All she knew was Laos, her "beloved homeland." And I hated Laos and what the Pathet Lao had done to my family, to all the Hmong. But that hatred was different. It had no face for my anger to latch onto. "Hatred" of the Pathet Lao was just something I repeated in my mind. Not in my heart.

My mind *and* my heart hated Grandma for humiliating me.

Chapter 6

I thought our journey had ended when the plane landed, but no family greeted us at the airport. We had to push through many reunited Hmong families wailing in happiness. Camera flashes popped in my eyes. A woman brushed past me and ran into the open arms of a Hmong man. Her children followed, shyly at first. Soon many Hmong were being swept into hugs. Some hadn't seen each other in ten years! Even the men were hugging. Where was *my* family? I wanted to jump over the velvety ropes into my cousins' arms. Where were See and Pa Cua? Why hadn't they come to welcome me? I bit my swollen lips to keep them from trembling.

Then a man called our names and led us down a wide and crowded corridor.

"They're sending us back!" Grandma said, panicked.

It couldn't be true. But if it were, why did *she* care? Maybe because she hadn't used the bathroom yet.

The man stopped at a seating area. "This plane goes to Providence," he said, pointing at a sign behind a desk.

It didn't sound right to me. I pointed to the ground. "Here. This Providence?"

The man shook his head. "San Francisco." He walked us over to a map that covered a whole wall. On the map in the plane, America had looked small. I could hold it in my hand. But now, America was five times my size. The man's finger followed a red line from Thailand up—ah, there were the Aleutians—then down to San Francisco. He traced a line from there to Chicago, then on to Providence. Now it sounded right, now that I could see it. And our plane sat right outside the window.

"To Providence," I said, with a nod of confidence.

I loved the warm, clean, roomy, perfumed bathroom. I could have stayed in it forever!

"Mai, hurry up," Grandma called.

"Just go back to our seats," I said. "We have some time."

After I used the toilet with its soft paper, I washed my body a bit in the sink with the squirty soap. A woman beside me pushed a button on the wall and put her hands under a machine. Warm air gushed out. I couldn't believe it! She left and it was my turn. No one was behind me, so I pushed the button again when the air stopped. Oh, it felt wonderful! I unbuttoned my blouse and let the air blow on my skin. The nozzle could move, and I turned it toward my face and hair. Wheee!

"Grandma, come see this!" I called, figuring she had probably stayed right by the door. I pushed the button again, throwing my hair forward so it covered my face. I did it one more time, then buttoned up and walked into the corridor.

I didn't see Grandma near the door. I looked left and right for her. It was so crowded and American people are so tall and wide I couldn't see anything. I ran to our seating area. She wasn't there. I stood on my seat and hollered, "Grandma!"

A pleasant voice came over a loudspeaker, saying something about a plane to Chicago. All of the people around me stood and picked up their bags. It would serve her right to be left here, I decided. But I couldn't leave her.

Oi! I grabbed fistfuls of my skirt and yelled, "Grandma?"

"May I help you?"

A dark-skinned officer appeared beside me. America had officers everywhere too? "Grandmother . . . ?" I said, and spread my hands, palms up.

The officer spoke into a radio, then walked over and talked with the flight attendant. When he returned, he said, "Don't worry. The plane can wait for a few minutes."

We walked back near the wide central corridor and the officer stood on a cart that looked like a *tuk tuk*. "Ah! I think I see her," he said. "Come, sit here." Off he drove, and the cart beeped along, people parting in front of us like brush in the jungle. And there was Grandma. She stood at a window display of embroidered and appliquéd shirts and hats.

"They use gum or pitch to stick it on," she said crossly. "It's not stitched. Nothing is really stitched. And they get money for this?"

I was too furious to speak, so I was glad the officer did.

"Grandma," he said, "your plane is leaving. Time to go."

Of course she didn't understand, but she got in the backseat of the cart.

Soon after we'd found our seats on the plane, a female voice came over the speaker. A woman pilot! Grandma would probably have a heart attack if I told her.

After we'd slanted up into the air, I felt even more secure. I could tell we were heading east, because we weren't flying over any oceans. Instead, we flew over boxes of land, and lakes that looked like giant spills of blue dye. It didn't seem that the farmers here needed to chop down trees and burn them in order to make good growing fields. They didn't need to make flat terraces on the mountainsides. Here there was plenty of land for us.

Soon a flight attendant came by and pointed out the Rocky Mountains. Their snowy slopes looked nothing like the steep limestone karsts of Grandma's "homelands." I thought about Pa Nhia back in Laos. Were the Communists leaving her and her family alone? Or did

Pa Nhia have to hide in mountain caves? My mind was running crazy with thoughts.

Grandma didn't try to talk with me. Good! She soon fell asleep, but I was too angry and too excited to sleep. The flight attendant handed out bags of peanuts! I'd eaten them only once before, when a Western worker in Ban Vinai tossed me a bag. I loved them so much, I took Grandma's bag too.

We stopped in Chicago and some passengers got off. Grandma gathered our things and stood in the aisle.

"Let's go," she said, nudging me.

"We don't get off here," I told her.

"I don't believe you. Everyone else is."

I spoke through my gritted teeth. "This is Chicago, not Providence. This is like the stop our bus made on the way to Phanat Nikhom."

Grandma nudged me again. "Ask. All the workers are standing near the front of the plane."

As I ducked and weaved my way toward the exit, I tried to calm down to be polite. I formed the question in English in my mind, then asked an attendant. "We go to Providence. We stay on?"

"That's right," he answered. "The plane will take on new passengers who are going to Providence too."

Smiling the whole way back, I told Grandma, "I was right."

I took my window seat again and watched all the busy workers on the ground. A little train of carts brought over huge square and rectangular cases, which then rode a belt up into the bottom of the plane. I couldn't believe Americans had so many belongings that they needed such cases. All the Hmong had were two or three white plastic sacks. And when the new passengers boarded the plane, they had even more bags! How did they expect to fit everything into such a small plane? A man stuffed his in a compartment over our heads, and I feared it would fall and crush us.

We took off again. The flight didn't take half as long as the others, and we didn't fly as high. I could tell we were getting close when I saw more cities spreading beneath us. I was getting good at this airplane flying. Maybe I could become a flight attendant, or even a pilot, like the lady who flew us from San Francisco.

Soon a man's voice came over the speakers, and lighted pictures came on over our seats. My ears began to feel taut as a pigskin drum. They had tightened in the other flights, but they hadn't hurt like this, even when I moved my jaw a hundred times. The plane bumped lower and lower through clouds, as if it were a bus descending a Thai mountain. This bumping and tipping hadn't happened either the other two times we landed. What was going on?

Grandma's hand squeezed mine on the armrest. I wanted to shake it off, but I didn't. The plane started to wobble. Its engines whined and belched. Suddenly, a loud roar beneath us made me pull my feet off the floor. A force pushed me forward. I had to brace myself against the seat in front of me. The rumble grew to a roar as the plane shuddered forward past planes standing still, past long flat buildings.

"Oh, please stop, stop the plane, stop, please," I said under my breath. The other people were looking around too, their eyes wide. The noise grew louder, and the shaking worsened. Suddenly, my body slammed against the back of the seat. Then all was quiet.

"Welcome to Providence," came a voice over the speaker.

I strained to hear any other words I knew. Did we have to rush off the plane before it exploded? Or put on the orange vests or air masks? The plane rolled easily toward the long flat buildings. I caught only a few more spoken words: "Cloudy . . . forty degrees . . . bags . . . gate."

Grandma stared straight ahead. Her left hand, white as cat claws, still clutched mine. Her right hand clutched at her heart. My heart was pounding too. I pulled my hand free and stood.

"It's over, Grandma. It's time to get off," I said.

She looked straight ahead and didn't budge.

"See? *Everyone* is leaving now," I added.

Did she think the plane would take her back to Laos if she stayed on board? Finally, when all the other passengers had left, she stood.

I hurried up the walkway into the airport, hoping to run right into See and Pa Cua's arms. I stopped at the velvet rope and searched for my cousins. Where were they? They were supposed to be here! Hugging me, crying with happiness. *Raum!* I felt so stupid!

When Grandma caught up with me, a man dashed out and threw his arms around her. I was startled.

"Niam," he kept saying. "Mother." His other words were lost in Grandma's sobs.

This was Uncle Ger? He was tall and thin the last time I'd seen him. Now he was my height and twice as wide. And . . . where had his hair gone?

A Western woman standing next to Uncle Ger spoke up. "Five years . . . that's a long time to be away from your family."

I backed away. Who was this stranger? How did she know such things about us?

Uncle Ger held his hands open to me, but I couldn't move to him. *"Maum,* daughter," he said, "you're growing up so beautifully."

I felt proud and embarrassed at the same time. Someone, almost a stranger to me, had called me daughter. But where were my cousins? *My* big reunion? "Uncle, where's Aunt Pa Khu and See and Pa Cua?"

"Oh, you mean Heather and Lisa. They have American names now."

Heather and Lisa? What strange names. Would I get a new name too?

As Uncle Ger led us through the airport, he explained why my cousins and Aunt Pa Khu hadn't come. "We don't have a car anymore. And we couldn't all fit in Miss Susan's car—oh," he said, gesturing to the Western woman with him. "Forgive me. This is Susan Clements. She comes from the church that's sponsoring you— helping you. She also teaches L.E.P. at your school, Mai."

I was confused by the English words. "Church"? "L.E.P."? Maybe there weren't Hmong words for these things.

Uncle Ger spoke in English to Miss Susan. I heard my name; then Miss Susan put out her hand and said, "How do you do?"

I remembered that greeting from PASS! And the English reply. "Fine, thank you. And you?" I said, trying to look her in the eyes. It was not disrespectful in America to do that. In fact, I had learned that it could be disrespectful *not* to look at the person you were talking to.

"Very good!" Miss Susan said, laughing. "School started two months ago, but you'll soon be my best student."

As we stepped through the doors, a whoosh of freezing air made me hunch up. Uncle Ger shook his head. "I'm sorry. I forgot that they don't give you enough clothing for the cold weather. Here, take my coat."

"This is 'cold'?" I asked, my teeth chattering.

"You think *this* is cold? It just turned November. The cold season hasn't even begun," Uncle Ger said with a laugh. "Tens of thousands of Hmong moved to Minnesota, where it's cold almost all year long. Mai, remember we sent pictures of Heather and Lisa playing in the snow? In Minnesota the snow comes up to my chin!"

Grandma's eyebrows arched in surprise. Playing in the snow didn't sound so bad, but I hated the cold immediately.

Uncle Ger settled me in the backseat of a tiny car, not a big car like my cousins wrote about. And it didn't go fast. It was just as cramped and bumpy as our bus ride in Thailand. At least no one was vomiting in this car. And the car made hot air inside to warm us all up.

Once we got going, Uncle Ger talked about the camp with Grandma, who was sitting in the front seat. Was so-and-so still there? Did such a rule pass? How was Yang Cher? Would he go back to Laos?

I didn't pay attention. Who wanted to think about the past? Instead, I looked out the window. There were lots of big flat buildings, like the ones near Bangkok. I watched trucks, big as planes, thunder by on the wide road. What could they possibly be carrying?

Trees blurred past. Where were the brilliant trees my cousins raved about—the green ones turned orange and yellow? The ones I saw were tall black-green spikes with sloping branches and others with bare branches that looked like twig brooms. Some buildings had flowers decorating their fronts. But they looked small, withered, faded.

Now and then, though, I caught sight of homes as big as mahogany trees, just as See and Pa Cua had described. Even the small houses looked more roomy than our hut in camp. I couldn't believe I'd soon live in such a home. With a carpet, an oven, and a refrigerator, too—the machine making heat right next to the one making cold.

I sounded out the numbers and words on the big

green signs above the road: 95, 295, and 10—that was easy. The words were harder, but soon I saw the word *Providence*.

I said it slowly. I liked how the word used all the parts of my mouth.

"Providence began as a refuge for people who wanted to worship God differently," Uncle Ger said. "The name means being taken care of by God—you know, Saub."

Miss Susan added, "The word 'providence' also means 'wisdom' and 'preparation for the future.'"

I understood and liked all the meanings. I wanted to have wisdom. And unlike Grandma, I had been ready for the future for years.

Soon the car slowed and left the highway. It weaved around other cars, waited beneath a tricolored light, then turned onto a narrower, quieter street. We passed neat square houses with browning grass and dead flowers.

"This is our neighborhood. It's just like a village," Uncle Ger said. "Almost all the Hmong in Providence live on these streets."

"Do you live in such a pretty house, son?" Grandma asked, pointing to a yellow one-story building.

Uncle Ger cleared his throat. "Not exactly. Those are 'family homes.' Only one family lives there. Someday I'll buy one. Maybe after two more years working in the jewelry factory."

The car stopped in front of a narrow but tall white building. The house had no front yard, just white cement with grass poking up through the cracks. No trees or flowers, even dead ones. Its layers of paint curled like corn husks, and its entranceway sagged in the middle.

"Well, here we are." Uncle Ger seemed embarrassed. Why? His house was huge! And it had so many windows.

"We rent the second floor," Uncle Ger said, climbing the stairs to the front door. "You'll live in the smaller space above us."

Miss Susan spoke for a bit, and Uncle Ger translated. "Yes, you were very lucky. Usually refugees have to live in a temporary house first. Since we're family, you were allowed to move into this open apartment right away."

I was grateful when the front door opened and we stepped into a place we wouldn't have to leave for a long, long time. And something smelled delicious! As we climbed the stairs and passed Uncle Ger's open door, I still didn't spot anyone. Where were See and Pa Cua? Didn't they want to welcome me?

We trudged up another set of stairs. I'd never seen so many stairs, except for the moving stairs in the airports. At the top Uncle Ger and Miss Susan stepped aside to let Grandma go first. She opened the apartment door, but loud yelling came pouring out at us. I jumped back.

Grandma quickly shut the door. She was shaking. "It's a mistake," she said. "They're angry. Maybe you have made a mistake, Ger. Maybe this isn't our new home."

Uncle Ger laughed. "Don't you recognize anybody? Everyone's here to welcome you!"

This time I threw open the door to our new home. A woman rushed over and hugged me so hard, I couldn't breathe. "Oh, Mai, you're finally here. Finally!" She pulled back, and I smiled to see Aunt Pa Khu. She hadn't changed at all. She had the deepest dimples I'd ever seen, and they were always busy because she smiled so much.

Two girls playfully shoved my aunt away and hugged me. I leaned back to look. American names or not, it was See, with the same flashing eyes, and Pa Cua, with a smile as wide and bright as a slice of coconut! Oh, I was so happy, I started crying like a baby. Five long years!

The girls pulled me into our apartment, and Grandma and I were swept up by one lady after another. Men, laughing, stood in groups of twos and threes and waved at us. Grandma looked confused but happy too. She kept laying her hands on the women's faces, then covering her own face and crying. My anger melted. How could I have hated her only hours earlier? I really didn't hate her—I just thought I did for a while. How shameful.

I turned to my cousins. Heather's fine black hair grew long on one side and short on the other. That looked strange, but maybe, I thought, lots of girls here wore their hair like that. Lisa's thick dark hair reached her backside. My own hair felt dirty and snarled. I couldn't wait to bathe.

"Look at you!" Heather said in Hmong. "We have got to get you something to wear."

I tried to smooth out the wrinkles in my yellow skirt. "What's wrong with this?"

They exploded into laughter. I joined in, nervously, trying to figure out what was so funny. I thought my cousins looked funny, dressed like the round-eyed men in Ban Vinai. Shirts with words or numbers on them, baggy jeans.

After they calmed down, Lisa stepped back and said, "Mai, you're so skinny, you could be a model."

I envied Lisa's healthy plumpness. She resembled her mother—round and soft. Heather's build was like her father's—well, the way he used to be, thin and muscular like strong rope. Both Lisa and Heather looked more like women than girls of fourteen and sixteen. Their chests had grown large. I felt ashamed of my skin and bones.

"I've been real sick," I admitted. "What's a 'model'?"

The girls laughed again. What had I said? Heather pulled a magazine from her purse and flipped to a brightly colored picture. I blinked in shock. A girl on a beach was wearing only tiny strips of checked cloth.

"That's a model!" Heather said, pointing to the yellow-haired girl. "And they make lots of money."

Money? A model couldn't be a bad thing, then. I bent over for a closer look. "Ah," I said, "lipstick!"

Heather laughed. "You sure learn fast, Mai!"

Soon I was passed around again from one Yang clan

member to the next and patted and cried over. Who were all these people claiming they knew me as a baby? I remembered a sense of family in the camp when I was about five or six. Many wives. Most husbands had died in the fighting. Many children, a few old ones. But the details and names and faces had faded, like the colors of a storycloth left too long in the sun. Well, at least everyone was speaking Hmong. My brain was tired from so much English in the last thirty hours. Tired of figuring everything out for Grandma too.

Aunt Pa Khu took me into the kitchen. The appliances were white with reddish-brown rust stains on them—not shiny and new like those in PASS. But my aunt worked them easily, twisting knobs on the stove this way and that. My eyes popped out when I saw a table sagging under the weight of many plates and pans of food. I had heard stories of the feasts the Hmong had had before the wars. But I had never seen, never smelled, never dreamed of such treats. I wanted to grab fistfuls from every bowl and stuff them into my mouth!

"I don't know how to begin," I said to Aunt Pa Khu.

She giggled, picked up a plate made of paper, and spooned on a bit of almost everything. She skipped one dish, saying, "I made this plain boiled chicken for Grandma. You probably want spicier food."

I shrugged. "I want it all!" Except for the rice. I had had enough rice to last me a hundred growing seasons. I pointed to one of the unfamiliar dishes. "What's that, Aunt Pa Khu?"

"Pork with, um, a little soy sauce, a little fish sauce, garlic, red pepper. This is fried shrimp—very delicious. And here is my specialty: egg rolls. Try!"

I picked up a brown papery tube and crunched into it. A million different textures and flavors exploded in my mouth. I had no words for the colorful vegetables and meat that spilled out onto my plate.

"You like my egg roll, huh?" Aunt Pa Khu said, beaming. "Here, dip it into the sauce."

I obeyed. My next bite zinged across my tongue, and I fanned my mouth. "Good chili!"

"Here, have a cold soda."

I drank a cup of bubbling orange liquid. Oh, it cooled my mouth and made fizzy feelings on my tongue.

With my heaping full plate, I walked over to Heather and Lisa. They were bouncing two little cousins on their knees.

"I can't believe the food!" I exclaimed between bites of the sweet shrimp. "Here, have some of mine. I have plenty to share."

Heather replied, "Thanks, but we ate already. Your plane was late and we were starving."

How could they be starving with so much food around? "Well, I'm going to eat everything on the table. What's your favorite?"

Lisa said, "We get pizza or hamburgers at school. We like them better than Hmong food."

"Sometimes we go out for Chinese food," Heather added.

"What could be tastier than what's on my plate? Anything more delicious would make me die of joy."

I couldn't wait to try everything my cousins had described in their letters, especially ice cream. But how could Americans eat it when it was so cold outside? Then again, we ate chilies when it was so hot, the birds couldn't sing.

After a while mothers began to leave with their youngest children. Some of the old men stayed behind. I had returned to the table for second and third helpings by then.

"Finish up already, Mai," Heather whispered. "We've got some plans for you."

I felt exhausted, especially after eating so much, but I wanted to be with them. Quickly I washed my plate in the sink, like we'd been shown in PASS. But it fell apart. Oh, no, I worried, what had I done?

Heather came up behind me. "What are you doing?"

"I'm sorry. I ruined the plate. I didn't—"

Heather shook her head and chuckled. "We throw these away, and the cups, too." She tossed my whole mess into a bag of dirty napkins and chicken bones.

"Wait, I can wash the fork," I said, digging it out of the bag. "We learned in camp that you can use plastic over and over."

"Forks, too," Heather ordered, pointing to the bag. "Go ahead, throw it back in. Good girl!"

As Heather and Lisa led me to the door, I kept looking back at that bag. There was so much uneaten food in there! We could make a soup from the bones, and if I washed all the plastic forks and knives, I could sell them as new.

Uncle Ger's voice interrupted my thoughts. "Where are you going?"

"Remember my test tomorrow, Father? We're meeting friends at the library to study," Heather said.

"Mai doesn't have anything to study," Uncle Ger said. "Besides, she should rest."

Heather whispered, "Say you're not tired, Mai."

I wanted to go so badly. I wanted to do everything they did. And there was Grandma, having a great time without me. She didn't need me. So why couldn't I go? I lowered my eyes and said, "Uncle Ger, I feel fine."

Uncle Ger stood up straight, his shoulders squared. "Mai, it is best for you to stay here. It's getting late, and you have been traveling for two days."

I pursed my lips, trying not to frown. I wished my cousins had the power to rescue me. But to go against Uncle Ger . . . ? He was the head of all of us now.

"It's all right, Mai," Lisa said with a shrug. "We'll go again tomorrow night, okay? Hey—you're with us for all the tomorrows."

I only half grinned. After all, I was being left behind again. Heather and Lisa didn't know how that felt.

Uncle Ger stepped out into the hall with the girls, leaving the door ajar. "You're not seeing Bobby, are you?"

Bobby? What kind of name was that? I wondered.

"No, Dad," Heather said. "Remember? I broke it off last month."

"All right, then. But it's a school night. Make sure you're back by nine o'clock."

After he came back inside and shut the door, I glanced around this huge apartment with slanted ceilings. Grandma was helping Aunt Pa Khu clean up. The men had gathered around a table, their heads together. I had no one left to talk to.

"Uncle?" I asked before he rejoined the men. "Could you please show me where I'll be sleeping?"

"Of course." He brought Grandma over and led us down a short hall. At the end a tall table had been set up already for our altar to the ancestors.

He opened a door on the right. "This is your room, Mai."

Across the hall was Grandma's room.

I didn't understand. "My own . . . room? Won't I be sleeping with Grandma?"

Uncle Ger chuckled. "You can, if you want. But having your own bedroom is a luxury. Not many Hmong have a special room of their own."

Grandma hung her head a bit. I did too. We'd never slept alone for as long as I could remember. As a baby in Laos I had slept safe between my parents, or with my mother when my father was away fighting. After my parents were killed and Grandma took me to Thailand, I slept with Grandma. It wasn't normal to sleep alone. Who would keep the *dab* away from me? Who would keep me warm? Especially here, where the windows wore icy grins.

Slowly I walked around the room, dragging my finger along a narrow dusty shelf that ran the length of the wall. I knocked on the walls, hollow like drums. I opened a door and met my first closet. I didn't even have clothes to put in it. The room had a wide seat built right into the window. My own window! Then I plopped down on a thick floor mattress. The bed didn't have the yellow roof my cousins' letters had bragged about, but it was softer than any mat I'd slept on. I pulled a flowery blanket up to my shoulders.

Grandma leaned against the door frame. "So, Mai, do you like the room? Do you want to stay?"

I lay back and eyed the rippling glass of the ceiling light. Such a big bed must hold many dreams. "Yes," I decided.

Grandma sucked in a quick breath, then turned her face away.

Uncle Ger said quietly, "Come, Niam, I'll show you your bedroom."

As my tired bones sank into the bed, all the confusion of the past months slid away. My first night of freedom! Blinking slowly, I glanced out my window. A nearly full moon tipped like a bowl, pouring out dreams of light.

Chapter 7

A foul odor tingled my nose and a sharp noise drilled into my ears. My first American morning had begun. I jumped up, ran out of the bedroom, and tried to find the noise. But it screamed from everywhere—bouncing off the walls—knifing my head from all directions.

I found Grandma in the living room, which was filled with smoke. She pointed to the ceiling, where a red button on a white disk was flashing. I had seen one of those disks in PASS, but I'd forgotten what it meant. I couldn't believe something that little could make such a hurtful noise.

"Make it stop, make it stop!" she shouted, holding her ears. "The spirit is screaming!"

I pulled a chair over and stood on it to reach the screeching thing. As I banged away at it with my fist, Grandma continued to cry and moan.

"It won't stop. It won't stop!" I yelled, before a coughing fit made me hunch over.

My aunt and uncle crashed through the doorway.

Uncle Ger, carrying a long red tube, ran through the smoky living room toward the kitchen.

"No, Uncle Ger." I pointed to the disk. "This is the problem here!"

But my uncle disappeared into the kitchen.

Aunt Pa Khu hollered, "Come on!"

She pulled me off the chair and led Grandma and me through the front door onto the third-floor landing. The noise chased us. Grandma put her fingers so deep into her ears, they could have met inside her head.

"I stopped the fire!" my uncle cried, swimming back into the smoky living room. "It's going to be okay. All clear!"

"Fix the alarm!" my aunt called.

We watched from the outer hallway as Uncle Ger got up on the chair, flipped the cover off the disk, and pulled out a small rectangular block. Magically, the beeping stopped, but Grandma didn't stop wailing. I couldn't stop coughing, and Heather and Lisa ran upstairs, adding to the confusion.

"Is everyone okay?" Lisa asked, coming to my side.

Uncle Ger stepped down from the chair and led us all back inside the apartment. He put his arm around Grandma, murmuring, "It's okay, it's okay, Mother. Everything will be fine."

Heather and Lisa opened all the windows as my aunt and uncle headed back into the kitchen. Grandma and I just stood in the middle of the living room, watching the smoke slither along the ceilings and out into the freezing air.

"Here's the culprit," Aunt Pa Khu announced, carrying out a charred pot at arm's length. "It *was* rice."

"We must have angered the cooking spirit," Grandma muttered.

Heather snickered and covered her mouth. "No, but somebody needs cooking lessons."

That was disrespectful. "Grandma didn't get *any* lessons at Phanat Nikhom," I explained. "Only I did. And our food was pretend food, plastic, and we had nothing to practice on at our quarters."

Heather mumbled, "Sorry."

The kitchen was a foamy white-and-black mess. Uncle Ger explained how the white stuff in the red tube put out the fire. While the grownups cleaned up the kitchen, Heather and Lisa pulled me down the hall into my new room.

"This is cool," Lisa said, sliding onto the window seat. She eyed Heather. "I wish I had my own room."

I sat next to her and wrapped my arms around myself.

"You're shaking!" Lisa exclaimed, squeezing me around my shoulders.

"How would you like to wake up to that shrieking?" I asked.

"Whose? Grandma's or the alarm's?" Heather said, stretching out on my mattress.

Lisa kicked her sister's foot. "Don't laugh," she scolded.

"I know it's a pain, Mai, but you really need that smoke alarm. Don't let Grandma keep the battery out, okay? Last year a fire killed a whole Hmong family in the middle of the night. They had removed the alarm's batteries, like Dad just did. They never woke up."

I shuddered. Our first day in America and Grandma had almost killed us!

Aunt Pa Khu knocked on the door and called the girls out. Then she and Uncle Ger showed us how to get to an outdoor staircase if we ever needed to escape. There was a small porch outside the back door, with a line for hanging clothes to dry.

"Let's go, girls," Uncle Ger said when they'd finished, "or you'll be late for school."

"School?" I said, walking with them to the front door. "Can I go too?"

Aunt Pa Khu answered, "Maybe in a few weeks. You and Grandma have a lot to do. In about an hour I'll be back with supplies and to show you around. We eat dinner at six o'clock. You will be eating dinner with us every night, won't you?"

I wanted to jump up and down. Real family dinners! Grandma nodded slightly and walked out of the room. I answered for her, "Of course."

"By-yee!" Heather and Lisa sang.

After everyone left, I heard Grandma's muffled sobs coming from the kitchen. I remembered my angry thoughts on the plane. Now I felt pity—not hatred—for Grandma. I hadn't expected her to act like a confused and lost child. I shut the windows on my way to the kitchen, where Grandma was sitting at the table, facing away from me. For a moment I stood behind her. Her shoulders quivered. I placed my hands on them and rubbed gently.

"The smoke was only a mistake," I whispered. "You didn't know."

"Of course I didn't know. Will I kill us with what I don't know?"

Feeling like the older, wiser one, I sat across from her. "Don't worry. You'll learn. I'll teach you. I'll help all I can."

Grandma dried her eyes, scanned the kitchen, then bowed her head again. "Everything's different, so difficult. Back home I had one room, one bed, one fire, one pot, one bag of rice. I never needed anything else."

"But here we can have so much more!" I said. "Didn't you like all the food and drinks last night?"

After a few moments Grandma lifted her face. "I'd like some more."

"Mmm, more egg rolls."

"That was the first chicken I've had in years," Grandma said, licking her lips. "I hope Pa Khu will have chicken again tonight."

"I bet she will. Now, I'm going to try taking a nice hot shower. When I'm done, I'll fix breakfast. But don't touch anything while I'm in the bathroom, okay? Do some *pa'ndau* or something."

"Don't worry," she said. "I won't touch a thing."

I undressed and stepped into the tub. I found the H and turned the faucet. Cold drops shot out from above, pelting my skin. "Oi!" Just as I reached for the other faucet, the cold water began to turn warm, then warmer. "Ah." But the next second the water was scalding me. I flattened myself against the tile wall and fumbled for the C faucet. After several wild twists I found the right mixture. Despite the warm water I shivered with shame. I, too, could kill us with what I didn't know.

Aunt Pa Khu returned, as she had promised. When a knock came at the door, I peeked through the peephole. Aunt Pa Khu's face looked as wide as a full moon, yet her body seemed so tiny. This peephole idea really could use some improvement! I thought with a giggle. I swung open the front door to see my normal-looking aunt clutching brown paper sacks and black bags.

"Beep, beep," she said, like a car. She struggled in and plopped the plastic bags on the floor. I followed her into the kitchen, where she set the paper bags down on the kitchen counter. "I took the morning off from work to help," she told us. "Let's put these groceries on shelves you can reach. Americans are so tall!"

We filled the cupboards with flour, rice, noodles, soy sauce, fish sauce, cooking oil. I saw the word "peanut" on a jar and opened it.

"Go ahead," said Aunt Pa Khu, grinning. "It was one of my girls' favorite foods when we first came."

I stuck my finger into the tan paste and tasted it. "Oh!

How delicious! Peanut butter," I pronounced, then took another fingerful.

We filled the refrigerator with meats, fruits, and vegetables, and stocked a closet with cleaning supplies. The only other place where I had seen such abundance was the PASS kitchen in Phanat Nikhom, and most of that stuff was plastic! I couldn't believe all this food was for us. I wanted to eat it all right away, before my dream could end.

"Now I'll show you around the apartment," said Aunt Pa Khu, "so you'll know how to work everything." She demonstrated the appliances and the bathroom fixtures. Then she spilled clothes and shoes out of the black bags on the living-room floor. "These were collected by people at our church," she said proudly.

I didn't understand and didn't care where or how they were collected. I just couldn't believe my eyes. "These clothes are a lot nicer than the ones we got in Thailand."

I tried on a pink coat and reached down to my knees to zip it. It was nice and warm, even though I felt as puffy as my mattress.

Grandma tried on a black fabric coat, which fell in slim folds to the tops of her new brown boots.

"The fashion show is over, ladies," said Aunt Pa Khu. "Now we must hurry to our appointments."

That morning's meetings reminded me of all the interviews we had had at Ban Vinai. We waited in crowded rooms, sat on hard chairs at big desks, signed papers we couldn't understand. I had a difficult time keeping up with my aunt's explanations, even though she translated everything into Hmong.

I finally understood how America would help us. Every month for the next six months, we'd get $500 to pay bills; about $250 worth of stamps to pay for food; and coupons to pay the doctor if we got sick. Even after I'd understood all this, I couldn't believe our luck. It had to be wrong! America was really giving us all this every month? Back in Thailand or Laos it would have taken Grandma and me more than a year to earn this kind of money. We were rich! No wonder everyone wanted to live here!

Aunt Pa Khu dropped us off at home in the early afternoon. I boiled bean thread noodles in broth for lunch, and I didn't burn the house down. Then the past few days caught up to me, and I lay down for a nap. But sleep was impossible. My mind raced with all the little choices I could make each day. Would we make chicken or pork to take downstairs for dinner? Noodles shaped like shells, like smiles, like tubes, like wheels? Would we like sweet red pepper or green pepper fried with the meat? I felt delirious again!

After a while I joined Grandma in the living room. She sat, hunched, on a footstool, stitching feverishly at a reverse-appliqué pattern of snail shells in bright pink and green. I let the soft green couch swallow me.

"That's pretty," I said. "What's it for? A ceremonial collar?"

Grandma tied a neat knot against the back of the material and snipped the excess thread. "A belt, maybe."

"I can't wait for New Year. It must be beautiful, because everyone here has money to buy or make *pa'ndau* with real silver charms and coins. Have you found out when it is? December's full moon should be early—because we'll have November's full moon tomorrow night."

Grandma put down her *pa'ndau*. "Mai, they already had New Year. Pa Khu told me."

"What?" I sat up, shocked.

"It's so cold and snowy here, and some people have to travel so far, that they celebrate New Year earlier. They had it last month, October."

I slumped back. I had pictured myself dancing in a new costume, eating and laughing with See and Pa Cua—Heather and Lisa. Maybe a boy would toss the ball with me for the first time. Now I would have to wait a whole year!

Grandma resumed stitching. "Don't be too disappointed, Mai. Pa Khu said her girls didn't even go this year. Heather hasn't been in years. They've *outgrown* it, Pa Khu said."

Why? The New Year festival was the biggest Hmong celebration. How could Heather and Lisa not even go?

At six o'clock I took Grandma downstairs to Uncle Ger's apartment. The door opened to a living room like ours, but they had a separate room for eating between the living room and kitchen. A huge television took up a whole wall. The wall across from it was almost all *pa'ndau*.

"Look, Grandma!" I exclaimed as we took off our shoes. "Your storycloth."

Uncle Ger walked over to the tapestry. "Everyone admires it. You have quite a reputation here, Mother. No one has seen such a finely detailed story of the wars in Laos—our villages in the Plain of Jars, Long Chieng air base, the tortures—"

"Enough, enough," Grandma said, waving her hand. "I don't stitch those stories anymore. I like patterns and folktales better. The war was a long, long time ago."

Uncle Ger shook his head. "It's still with many of us. We need *pa'ndau* like this so Hmong will never forget."

"Forget what?" Heather said, walking into the room.

"The war—Oh, my God!" Uncle Ger shouted. "What did you do to your hair?"

I caught my breath as I spotted an orange streak on the long side of Heather's shiny black hair. It made her look like a tiger.

Heather shrugged. "I just put a little color in it."

"Well, take the little color out!" Uncle Ger yelled. "No daughter of mine is going to look like a gangster drug addict."

I didn't understand the English names Uncle Ger called Heather. But the flames in his brown eyes told me the names weren't nice. Grandma looked ready to rub the orange out of Heather's hair, as she had done with my lipstick. False hair, false thoughts? No. . . .

Heather stood there, alone. I wished I were strong enough to stand beside her.

"I can't take the color out, Daddy," Heather explained. "It takes a week to wear off. I'm sorry. I guess I didn't understand the directions on the package."

Uncle Ger's lips blew out with exasperation. *"Tsov tom!"* he seethed, then stormed through a swinging door into the kitchen.

I thought things would calm down, but then I heard Aunt Pa Khu cry out, "Not scissors again! Please don't cut her hair. The color will go away. Please!"

Scissors! My eyes flew to Heather, who lifted her chin, daring her father to come back into the living room. The kitchen door swung less and less, and finally stopped. Behind it the argument continued, muffled.

Soon Aunt Pa Khu, her face blotchy, carried food out. She nodded at everyone to sit at the table. Grandma and I waited to see which chairs were taken. Then we took two seats against the wall, across from Heather and Lisa. The egg rolls and meat tasted as delicious as the night before, but I couldn't enjoy them. Clinks of spoons and forks stood in for talk.

The silence made me more nervous, so I tried asking some questions.

"Lisa, how many children are in your group at school?"

"Well, there are about eight hundred in the ninth grade."

"Eight *hundred?*" I glanced at Heather, hoping she'd

join the conversation. But she kept her eyes on the ceiling as if she were searching for a particular star. "How do they all fit under the roof?"

Lisa laughed. "There are many classrooms. One teacher teaches about twenty students at a time. You'll see."

As I helped Lisa wash the dishes later, Aunt Pa Khu and Heather were whispering together. Aunt Pa Khu's eyes brimmed as she cupped her daughter's chin. Heather looked away.

When we'd cleaned everything up from dinner, my cousins pulled me toward the door.

Uncle Ger growled, "Where are you going and who will you be with?"

"Shopping with some friends from school," Lisa softly replied. "They've been asking to meet Mai."

"Hmong girls?" Uncle Ger asked. "With Hmong hair?"

Lisa nodded.

"No boys, Heather?"

Still facing the door, Heather shook her head slowly.

"Okay. It's Friday night. You can have until ten."

I fetched my pink coat from upstairs, then met my cousins on the front steps of the house. After the tension in the apartment, I gulped the fresh cold air with relief.

"Hurry," Heather said, landing on the street. "We were supposed to meet Bobby on the corner of Elmwood and Warrington twenty minutes ago."

Bobby? That strange name again. "Is Bobby American?"

Without slowing, Heather explained, "Bobby Fuentes is my boyfriend."

"Didn't you tell Uncle Ger—"

"Mai, you've got a lot to learn, okay? In America my father has no right to tell me who I can like or dislike. I'm sixteen years old, after all! When he asked me last month, I told him the truth—that I hadn't broken up with Bobby—and he hit me. Can you believe it? And you saw how crazy he gets over something as little as hair color."

"Heather," Lisa said, "you knew damn well how crazy he'd get about your hair, but you did it anyway."

"So what? Lots of girls *and* boys dye their hair. I'm not breaking any law! At least I didn't pierce my nose and let all my spirits leak out."

I had seen women in the airports with all kinds of metal stuck in their faces. How could they destroy such beauty?

I was relieved to see Lisa shake her head in disapproval of her sister. That meant that Heather must have done something wrong. And maybe Heather's explanation of what an American girl could do was false. Or not entirely true. A father would know what was best for his family, right? Parents always told their kids who they could be with, what they could do. If the kids disobeyed, shouldn't they get hit? I struggled to hide my confusion.

Heather and Lisa turned a corner, pulling me with them. "In America, Mai," Heather continued, "you can get the police after your father if he hits you. Of course, I would *never* do that! But why put up with it? So I tell little fibs now and then to make Dad happy, and I don't get a black eye."

Heather got away with disobeying *and* lying to her father? I didn't think I could ever do that. "The rules here are very different," I muttered.

"There are no rules in America," Heather said.

"You wish. . . . Hey, there they are!" Lisa said, smoothing her hair.

As I was trying to make sense of what I had just heard, my cousins slowed to a walk that made their hips slide from side to side. What did they do that for? Ahead, two boys stood under a light on a post. Ghostly breath came from their mouths, and a pulsing chant blared from a huge radio at their feet.

"Hey, great stripe!" yelled the bald, dark-skinned American boy.

"Thank you. I'm glad somebody other than me likes it." Heather loudly kissed him on the lips. "Mai, this is Bobby," she yelled over the song.

I smiled a little, feeling my chin fall to my chest. This guy stood much taller than the men I knew. I could see why Heather liked him. He was handsome. A square jaw, a broad brow, and deep brown eyes.

"Hey," he said to me.

Hey? What was this "Hey?" How come I never

learned this greeting in PASS? I tugged my puffy coat tighter and glanced where Bobby's arm pointed. A Hmong boy!

"That's Lue."

Even though Lue was Hmong, he said "Hey" too.

I lifted my eyes and tried it. "Hey."

Lisa slung her arm around my shoulder and said, "Good!" in English. Then she whispered in Hmong, "Lue says when he finishes high school next year, Mom and Dad can negotiate our marriage. But we have to keep our relationship a secret till then. Or else Daddy will make us marry now, and Lue will be mad at me."

I nodded, though I wondered what finishing school had to do with marriage. Lue whipped his hand around and brought a cigarette to his mouth. Bobby gave one to Heather and asked me if I wanted one.

"No," I said, waving the smoke from my face. Back at camp I had once picked up a stub somebody had thrown down, and sucked on it. I coughed for hours!

While they smoked and chatted fast in English, I stole looks at them. Lue had high Hmong cheekbones, and his hair was cropped so short, it stood on end. He was the same height as Lisa, a bit taller than me. He had on jeans and a huge black top that had a hood and a pocket in the middle for his hands. The word "Patriots" went across his chest. What did that mean?

Bobby had on a jacket, satiny as the coat of a wet water buffalo. He wore light-blue jeans that were almost white at the knees. And big boxy sports sneakers that weren't laced up. Heather and Lisa seemed to match them, with jeans, sneakers, and short puffy jackets.

Bobby said something and everyone followed him to a small rusty car. Heather sat in the front, separated from Bobby by a lever. I crawled into the back, as I'd done in the car from the airport. Lue followed me, then Lisa. I shivered to feel Lue's muscular arm and leg against me. The only other time I'd been this close to a man was with that rapist soldier in Phanat Nikhom. I folded my arms over my chest and squeezed my legs together. But Lisa's cheerful babbling in Hmong soon made me relax.

Lue drew a package from behind his feet and offered me a bottle. "Want a beer?"

"It's like Singha beer in the camp," Lisa explained. "You could try."

I tipped the bottle. My lips puckered as the bitterness fizzled on my tongue. I shook my head and handed the bottle back. Bobby's round eyes gleamed in the mirror at me. "That's okay, Mai. I don't drink either."

"I'll take hers," Heather said, exchanging her already empty one.

I didn't understand why my cousins drank beer. Were they trying to go crazy like those drunks and opium addicts in camp? Hmong despised people like that. When the Thai soldiers drank beer, they picked fights with the refugees or worse. Pa Nhia had said that the soldiers who had dirtied her were drunk. Once when I was collecting bottles for my mosaic, I'd seen a Hmong man drinking the last drops—flies and all—out of the empty bottles in the garbage. Disgusting!

Bobby kept driving around slowly. I wondered if we were ever going to go shopping. At each red light he and Heather kissed until the car behind us honked. And Lisa and Lue counted how many seconds it took for the car to honk. Once when there were no cars behind us, Bobby and Heather kissed the whole time—even when the light changed colors all over again. Lisa and Lue kissed too, but they didn't wait for any red lights.

What was I supposed to do? I freed a thread from my cuff and wound it around my finger. At first I couldn't look at the kissing. Then I couldn't help watching it. The sight made my scalp tingle, yet I couldn't even imagine doing it myself.

Finally, we stopped at a store. But all they bought was a small roll of candy. We stood alongside the store, and my cousins and the boys talked with some other kids and smoked and drank some more. After her fourth, I lost count of how many beers Heather drank. I kept trying not to yawn. My face must have looked strange, though, so I let the yawns go and covered my mouth. At last we got back into the car and Bobby drove for a while longer. He stopped in front of a green house the same shape as ours.

"Come on. Let's go," Lisa said in English.

"But our house is white," I said.

"I can't let Daddy hear or see Bobby's car," Heather explained. "We only have to walk half a block."

I frowned, feeling anxious.

"See you later, Mai," Bobby called.

See? "See" was Heather's Hmong name. And "You" was a Hmong name too. I was confused all over again. I did what I had been doing all evening. I shrugged and smiled a little.

On the way home Heather pressed a small white circle into my hand. "It's candy. You suck on it," she said, pulling her jacket tight.

It tasted like a mouthful of mint leaves.

"It's so Daddy doesn't smell the smoke and beer on my breath. We could get in trouble. We're not old enough to drink beer in America."

She chose now to tell me this? I was not only disobeying Uncle Ger, I was breaking an American law my second night here! And Heather had said there were no rules in America. What could I believe?

Heather and Lisa stumbled noisily upstairs, saying "Shush!" to each other over and over. When they reached their landing, Heather faced me. I thought she was going to say something like "We're so happy you're finally here." But no. She crept so close, I could smell her breath. Mixed with the beer, it smelled like rotten mint leaves.

"If anyone—like Grandma or my father—asks what we did tonight, you say this: 'We just walked around the mall with a bunch of girls and talked.' If they ask what we talked about, say, 'I don't know. They talked mostly in English.' Got it?"

I thought I understood her, but I didn't want to. She must have read my face.

"Look," Heather said. "I don't want you to get into trouble, that's all."

I felt a strange mixture of gratitude and anger. Why had they gotten me involved in something they knew was wrong? It *was* sort of fun, and nobody got hurt. But what if we were caught?

Going upstairs, I tried to calm myself so Grandma wouldn't suspect anything. She was probably too worried about her own troubles. She was probably making charms to keep away the bad smoke-alarm spirits. But when I opened the door to our apartment, it was Uncle Ger's voice I heard.

"Have a good time?" he asked.

I tried to let my breath out slowly. "Yes, but I'm so tired still. I'm going to bed. Good night."

In my room, safe behind the closed door, I undressed quickly and crawled under the covers. A few moments later I heard one set of footsteps coming down the hall. Good, Grandma was going to bed. Then my own door-knob twisted and a blade of light sliced the room in two.

"Mai?" came Grandma's voice. "Your uncle Ger wants to know if Heather met a boy named Bobby tonight."

I was shocked! I struggled to keep my eyes shut but not pinched tight. My body stayed still as a tree trunk.

How could I answer? Uncle Ger might beat Heather. Lisa, too. And me! Would he cut the hair off all of us? Just because we went with boys, and one of them was American? If I told the truth, Heather and Lisa would hate me. They'd never let me go anywhere with them again.

I felt tired from all this thinking. I just wanted to sleep. In my mind I ordered Grandma to please go away, to tell Uncle Ger to go home, to say he should ask his own daughters. Let *them* lie. They were used to it.

Lie . . . that's what it was. I had never lied before.

Heather's pretty face, complete with orange-streaked hair, came clear to my closed eyes, and I heard her voice: "I tell little fibs now and then to make Dad happy, and I don't get a black eye." And from a lifetime ago, Miss Sayapong's words came back: "Many lies have put you here. Allow me a tiny harmless lie to help get you out." Lies could help, I reasoned. They weren't always wrong. It would be okay for me. One tiny harmless lie, only one.

I had finally parted my lips to answer "no" when Grandma closed the door. "I guess she fell fast asleep," I heard her telling Uncle Ger. "It's been a long journey."

And it's not over yet, I realized.

Chapter 8

The next morning I could not eat breakfast. I stayed in the shower for a long time, because I knew Grandma wouldn't bother me there. This hot and cold water coming out of one faucet scared her. And the steam reminded her of the smoke from the burned rice. She preferred to stand at the sink and wash, the way we had to stand at the basins in Ban Vinai. The hot shower numbed me, taking away my fear of facing Heather and Uncle Ger again.

Soon after I turned the faucet off, I heard Heather in our living room. She sounded like a happy bird, chirping away to Grandma about school and the people at church who gave us clothes. Maybe she wasn't mad at me after all!

When I entered the living room, Heather turned her bloodshot eyes on me. Grandma kept doing *pa'ndau*. Heather grabbed my hand and pulled me back the way I had come. "Mai, let's see all the clothes the church brought! Maybe we can trade."

Everything was okay! She wasn't mad. I felt light,

suddenly, like the moment a shower ends and you're still in the steamy cocoon. I rushed ahead and dragged the black plastic bag from the closet.

"Look at this!" I exclaimed, putting on a blue blazer. "Isn't it beautiful?"

Heather made her eyes go around in their sockets. "Oh, Mai, I didn't come up here to look at the crappy clothes people throw away."

I lowered my eyes and fingered a brass button. I didn't want to ask her why she had come up.

Heather put her hands on her hips. "The first words out of Daddy's mouth this morning were: 'You saw Bobby, didn't you?'" she whispered harshly. "Did you say anything to my father last night?"

Heather's accusation took my breath away. "No! Honest!" I blurted.

"Shush!" Heather closed the door and stepped right up to my face. "What did you tell my father? What I told you to say?"

My own face twitched. All I could see was Heather's orange streak flashing like the coat of a stalking tiger. "I didn't tell him anything! Grandma asked me about Bobby after I'd gone to bed, and I couldn't make myself answer. Really, I couldn't. I was afraid Uncle Ger would cut my hair too. Grandma must have thought I was asleep. So they just left."

"Oh," Heather said. The furrows in her high forehead faded, and she stepped back. I couldn't believe how she could change so fast—one moment wild, the next moment tame. "Because I told Daddy our story, the one I told you to say. And he acted like he didn't believe me. He waved his hand like he was shooing a fly."

I inhaled shakily. Heather's explanation hadn't calmed me at all.

"I'm sorry, Mai," she went on. "I didn't mean to accuse you. Daddy makes me nervous. I'm always afraid he's going to hit me. You've seen him—how angry he gets."

I nodded, thinking that maybe Uncle Ger should hit Heather *more*. Hmong children never disobeyed. From what I saw last night, I guessed American children did all the time. It seemed as if nobody was in charge of an American family. That would be scary, having no one to protect me. I hoped Uncle Ger hadn't become like that.

"Would you look at these?" Heather said, pulling checkered slacks from the bag.

I fingered the thick cloth. "They're pretty, and they'll keep me warm."

"What?" Heather threw the pants at a wastepaper basket. "I can't believe people expect us to wear this junk. I wish they'd give us only the clothes that don't fit them anymore—not the stuff that's way out of style."

I had never owned pants before. I took the checkered pair out of the basket, and said, "Heather, it's freezing here. And I don't have anything else to wear."

"*Ntsej muag!* If you wear those, kids will laugh at you. 'Fresh off the jet,' they'll say. You need to go shopping," Heather stated. "For school clothes."

"Shopping like last night? Not again."

Heather laughed. "No, this time we'll really go. To the Emerald Square Mall for the right clothes. You got money yesterday, didn't you?"

I remembered the thick envelope of green bills and coupons Grandma and I had received. I'd never seen so much money in all my life. There would be plenty to buy something really nice to wear. Something no one had worn before. Something of my own.

"Yes," I said. "Let's go!"

In the kitchen I pulled out a drawer and opened the envelope. "How much will we need?"

Heather reached over and counted out ten twenty-dollar bills. "This will do it . . . for starters. Let's go."

As we headed for the door, Grandma called out, "Where are you going?"

"Shopping," replied Heather.

"Is that all girls do in America?" Grandma asked.

I giggled. If Grandma only knew.

"Yup," Heather chirped, pulling me through the door.

Lisa joined us on the busy Saturday sidewalk. Hmong women had infants strapped to their backs like in Thailand. They pulled around shopping carts filled with vegetables and groceries. Their children, bundled in jackets and hoods, chased each other from house to house. Outside the small shops, Hmong men stood with their heads together. Uncle Ger was right. It did feel like a real village. Not a locked warehouse of people. In camp people sat around all day with nothing to do.

Lisa waved to some girls her age across the street. "That's Chee and Deb."

Deb, I repeated to myself. Another American name. "Heather, Lisa, why do some Hmong change their names? Why did *you* change?"

Heather answered first. "Because in English 'See' means too many different things. It sounds like a letter of the alphabet, and a word meaning ocean. It also means 'look.' So every time someone would say 'see,' I'd jerk my head around like an idiot. Plus, if you're 'seeing' someone, you're boyfriend and girlfriend. Like I'm 'seeing' Bobby."

"Oh . . . okay," I said. "Lisa, how about Pa Cua?"

Lisa shook her head. "Horrible! In English, the name sounds like a sneeze. Every time someone would say 'Pa Cua,' some wise guy would snicker, 'Bless you.'"

I nodded. That would be embarrassing. I hoped I wouldn't be teased about my name and have to change it. I liked my name. Mai meant "precious."

"Would you like a new name too?" Lisa asked.

I shook my head and giggled.

"Oh, come on, Mai!" Heather said. She ran ahead of me and danced backward as Lisa and I walked forward. "How about Melissa—Melissa Sue? In the southern states all the girls have two first names."

"Why?" I asked. "Couldn't their parents make up their minds?"

"Probably something like that." Lisa laughed. "How about a royal name for this little refugee. Victoria? Diana? Anastasia?"

"Or an old-fashioned name like Gertrude or Hilda?"

"I can't even pronounce all those names!" I said. "I like 'Mai.' Short, simple 'Mai,' just like me."

As we chattered in Hmong on the bus to the mall, I expected people to stare at us, at our mouths, at our difference, the way the soldiers in Phanat Nikhom had or the people in the airports. Or that apple vendor. Did people on the bus think we were *Meo* too?

I caught myself staring at people, whose skins ranged from whitest coconut to darkest soil. I made out two other languages besides English and Hmong. The bus was packed as tightly as our bus from Ban Vinai. I didn't want so many strangers so close to me. It scared me a little. I huddled with Lisa by a silver pole. The pole reflected the other people, so I could watch them secretly. The pole made their bodies look funny sizes, like the peephole did. That made me feel better.

Once inside the place they called the mall, I stepped to a clear railing and gasped. The floor seemed to fall away beneath my feet. A garden bloomed in the middle of the building, and a fountain sprang from the center. Mothers and fathers sat around it, while their children ran in circles. Hundreds of stores on two different floors lined the wide corridors.

"Cool, huh?" Lisa said.

"Cool," I repeated, liking the *oooo* sound in my mouth.

"You won't believe this, Mai," Heather said. "In Minnesota, where lots of Hmong live, one mall has a roller coaster in the middle and all kinds of rides."

"What's a roller coaster?"

"I know!" Lisa said. "It's like that bus ride from Ban Vinai—up, down, upside down, and all around."

I remembered the flutters and dizziness—half from the ride itself, but half from excitement.

"Don't people get sick?" I asked.

"Yes!" Heather was grinning. "Americans actually love it."

I shook my head. I had already had enough upside downs and spins and plunges in the past year. I'd never go on such a ride.

Lisa linked her arm through mine and said, "Come on—our favorite store is this way."

We started walking, but a tangy aroma soon had my stomach cramping with hunger. "What is that food? Can I have it now?"

Heather smiled slyly. "Sure, but we won't tell you what it's called until you've eaten it."

I thought about the beer and wondered if Heather would get me in trouble again. But from the restaurant doorway I saw a father feeding bits of the food to his baby boy. It reminded me of Yia and Koufing. I had one more question: "Do we have enough money?"

"Of course!" Lisa said. "Let's go in."

We sat, and Heather whispered to a young woman carrying a tray, the waitress. Soon the woman brought over some drinks and a red-and-whitish circle that was almost as big as our table. I leaned over and inhaled the spicy fragrance, then picked up a piece and bit in. Chewy, oozy, spicy, crunchy all in one bite! When I opened my eyes, Lisa and Heather were staring at me, their eyebrows arched.

"Well, what do you think?" Heather asked in English.

"Hot!" I said, pointing to the roof of my mouth.

"Ha! What's the food?" Lisa said.

"Pissa!" I said, bits of it flying out of my mouth.

Lisa laughed so hard, she put her head on the table.

Heather slapped the table over and over. "Piss! Pissa!" she said, repeating my English answer. "Excuse me, waitress, can I have a pizza with extra piss on top?"

I started laughing too, because they were crying now and couldn't get any words out.

Lisa kept taking deep breaths, and finally she calmed down. "Mai, my oh Mai," she said, still chuckling. "Oh, my, that was good. Listen, Mai, the word is said 'peet-za.'"

"Peet-za," I repeated. The Hmong had no word for pizza. Before the war, who even knew pizza existed? "Now, what was so funny about pissa?"

Heather told me about the word in English that sounded like "pissa," and we all laughed hard again. Soda bubbles went up my nose, and sauce drooled down my chin.

In between laughing fits I ate four slices—what a pig! I was afraid the pizza would be taken from me. I couldn't believe it when Lisa said we could take the rest of it home in a box.

"Can I carry it?" I begged.

"Oh, Mai," Heather said, elbowing me. "You are such a refugee!"

I shrugged. She could call me anything while the warm box was in my hands and I wouldn't care. Pizza now meant even more to me. It had magical powers to bring cousins together.

As we walked around in the mall, I couldn't take my eyes off everything there was to buy: black-and-white puppies, fake hair on fake heads. And oi! Cushions that made the sound of human gas! Who would want something like that? Americans could be very strange.

We entered a store and were surrounded by shelves of pants. Heather pulled me over to a corner and started holding pairs in front of me.

"I still can't believe how skinny you are, Mai," she said. "I have to starve myself to stay slim."

"That's because there's no pizza in Ban Vinai!" I joked. "Now I'll get good and chubby."

"Don't you dare!" Lisa said, patting her own round hips. "Americans are real mean to heavy people—especially girls."

I didn't think that was very nice of Americans.

Skinny women can't be strong women, strong mothers, strong workers.

In the dressing room my cousins paired my jeans with a plain black shirt with long sleeves and a high neck. My cousins chose shirts just like it so we could be triplets. The sales clerk let me keep the outfit on after Heather told him they were my first American clothes. "Cool," he said. The shoe clerk in the next store also let me keep my Nikes on. I almost tripped in them, they were so bulky and heavy. And I didn't know how to work the laces. In Thailand I either went barefoot or wore rubber sandals.

As we headed to the bus stop, I caught Lisa frowning at Heather. Finally Lisa asked her, "Where did you get the money for all this?"

Heather rolled her eyes. She did that a lot. "I guess you were too little to remember. When we first got to America, the church and the government gave us a bunch of money to get started. This is only a little part of what Grandma and Mai got."

"Right," I said. "You should see how fat the money envelope is."

"Then ... I guess it's okay," Lisa said.

Dark clouds had moved in by the time I got home, wearing my new clothes and carrying the pizza. I felt so proud of how I looked that I walked the way Heather and Lisa did, my hips sliding back and forth. I ran up the stairs and burst into our living room.

"Hi, Grandma! How do I look?"

Still sitting, doing needlework, Grandma peered up at me, then frowned. "How do you look? Like your sloppy cousins," she muttered. "How much did the clothes cost?"

I twirled and sang, "I don't know."

Suddenly, wind and rain slammed against the windows. Grandma brushed past me into the kitchen. She took the envelope out of the drawer and gasped. "Almost half of it is missing!"

I stopped spinning. "Don't worry, Grandma. We still have plenty left, and Heather said we'll get more money next month."

"Miss Best Student, figure out how much *plenty* we have left." Grandma rattled a paper with pictures and numbers at me. "Last night, when you girls went shopping, Ger made a budget for us. See how your new American clothes fit now!"

My mouth went dry as the rain came even harder. I heard gurgling, and I couldn't tell if it was my stomach or the drains outside. At the top left of the page Grandma handed me, I read the figure $500. Beneath that: the figure $350 lined up with a picture of a house; $80 lined up with a light bulb and a heater; $30 lined up with a faucet with water coming out; $20 lined up with a telephone; and $20—not $200—lined up with a happy face.

I felt wobbly, as if I were riding the roller coaster Americans liked so much. I ran to the bathroom and threw up pizza. It had burned my mouth earlier at the mall. Now it burned my throat with acid. When I had gotten sick in Thailand, I could always count on Grandma to comfort me. She would rub my back or my stomach, bathe me with a cool rag, chant to the spirits, clean my mess. This time she did not follow me into the bathroom.

After a few minutes I cleaned up the toilet, washed my face, and brushed my teeth. I rinsed my new clothes, now soiled. Then I dressed in the checkered pants Heather had wanted to throw away and a stained blue shirt that said "University of Rhode Island."

When I shuffled into the kitchen, Grandma said, "You'll have to get the money back."

And how was I supposed to do that? I couldn't make a fool of myself with Heather and Lisa. I certainly couldn't get to the mall by myself. Plus the store would never take the clothes back after I'd worn them. Thrown up on them! Returning the clothes would be like handing back the shell of a rambutan after I'd eaten the fruit.

"I can't get the money back," I finally replied.

"Heather and Lisa must help you," Grandma said, sitting at the kitchen table.

I shook my head.

"They have to!" Grandma insisted. "I will make them!"

I pleaded, "Please don't. Here you have friends from Thailand and Laos. I have nobody but them!"

"They are my own grandchildren. But they are not good for you!" Grandma said, meeting my gaze.

Instinctively, I lowered my eyes. But I didn't want to. I wanted to look her right in the eye and argue.

She continued to rant. "They must have put you up to this. I don't like what has happened to my See, especially. This 'Heather' has no truth in her bones. Ger should lock her up until he finds a strong-willed man to marry her."

That was an argument I didn't want to touch. I sat at the table and bowed my head. "I'm sorry, Grandma. I didn't know. I had no idea clothes cost so much. Everything costs so much. Five hundred dollars sounded like a fortune. And now . . ." I wrung my hands under the table and leaned forward. "Please don't make me return the clothes. I'll make the money back somehow. I—I— I'll sell my *pa'ndau*."

Grandma heaved a sigh that sat like a fog between us. At last she said, "I can sell mine, too. Ger said there's a fair next Saturday. But who knows what our work will fetch? Will it be enough? All the women and girls must do *pa'ndau,* so who is left to buy it?"

I glanced around the kitchen for more answers. I jumped up and turned off the light. "Maybe we can spend less on lights, food, heat."

"We'll have to," Grandma said, leaning on the table as she stood. She scuffed into the living room. I followed, shivering as if we'd already shut off the heat. "Well, Mai, get to work. The more *pa'ndau* we have to sell, the better. Ger said . . ."

Uncle Ger! I panicked. What if he found out about

the money? What would he do? Take those scissors and shred the new clothes? Drag us back to the store? "Grandma, please don't tell Uncle Ger about the money. It's all my fault, more than my cousins'."

Grandma shook her head sadly. "This time I won't tell him. Ger has enough problems with those girls. But there'd better not be a next time."

I nodded, relieved by her mercy. "Thank you."

"For this I want no thank-you," Grandma muttered. Then she plunged her hand into her bag of threads and cloth. I sat at her feet the way I'd sat as a child. And together we worked long into the night.

The day before the craft fair Heather called for me. I dropped my *pa'ndau* and stepped out into the hall with her. "You still do that embroidery stuff?" she asked.

"Of course. Don't you?"

Heather shook her head. "Nobody does! Lisa and I haven't done it in years. It takes too long, plus it cramps my hand. . . . Mai, we're all going to the library. Want to come?"

"Are you going to study?"

Heather tilted her head and sang, "Maybe."

Maybe not, I said to myself. I had never seen Heather with a book, nor Lisa. "I don't know." I wrung my hands and shook out my own cramps. I'd been working so hard this past week, I had scarcely seen my cousins. I missed them. I wanted Heather take me to new places and show me exciting things. And I liked the way Lisa treated me like a little sister. It was the way Yia had spoken to me in Phanat Nikhom, gently, patiently.

"Mai!" came Grandma's voice from inside. "I need you."

I frowned and told Heather, "I can't, sorry. We have to sell a lot tomorrow. We need the money real bad." As if Heather didn't know.

"Okay, your loss." And she left, swinging her hips, down the stairs.

I closed the door and went back to work on a story-cloth border of triangles. In the silence I pictured my cousins kissing their boyfriends—their heads turning gently like leaves in the breeze. Then, somehow, the boys turned into monstrous soldiers. "Oi!" I sucked the finger I'd just stabbed.

Grandma spread *pa'ndau* on the floor. "Let's see what we've got."

I inventoried the pieces we'd sell: a vest, three belts with imitation French coins, six reverse-appliqué squares, four small storycloths, and three the size of our kitchen table.

"I wonder how much money they will fetch," Grandma said. "In Thailand I would have known how to price all of it. But here?"

"Don't worry," I said. "We'll ask Uncle Ger tomorrow."

The next morning Uncle Ger drove us to their church.

"Is this where our clothes came from?" I asked. "Is church some kind of store?"

Uncle Ger laughed a bit. "Well, money is exchanged here, but that's not the real reason we come to church. It's a holy place where nice people can gather to meditate, pray, sing. I'll bring you soon on a Sunday, and you can learn more."

Uncle Ger led us under the church to a long hall filled with tables. We set up our *pa'ndau* display near the other Hmong artists, who were all elderly. I didn't see one girl my age. As we finished, a man in a black suit and white collar called Uncle Ger away.

The customers trickled in. I glanced at the other displays and hoped ours would attract the most customers. Strangely, I'd never felt competitive with the women and girls in the Widows' Store at Ban Vinai. Perhaps because we knew we'd be fed in the camp. We didn't have to worry about things like heat and rent. Here in America we needed all the money we could get.

A round American lady with skin the color of cotton strolled over to our table. She flipped through our storycloths as if they were pages in a book. She ran her fingers over the stitches and whistled softly. She smiled and said something in English about not sewing buttons.

Grandma looked at me as if I could tell her what the American lady was saying. I shrugged, then simply smiled at the lady.

The lady selected a large stitched folktale, "Saub and His Fire." She said, "I don't see a price. How much?"

I understood her question. I whispered in Hmong to Grandma, "What did Uncle Ger say about prices?"

"Nothing yet," she replied. "But he said he'd be right back."

When the woman glanced over at the other displays, I couldn't keep from winding some embroidery thread around my finger. Would we lose our first customer? Maybe our *only* customer? "Grandma, I have to say *something*."

Grandma wagged her finger. "Wait until Ger returns."

"We don't know when that will be. Can you ask the other women?"

Grandma looked over at them nervously. "No, I don't know them."

The lady arched her eyebrows at us and tilted her head. When she got no reply from us other than my stupid smile, she shrugged. She placed the *pa'ndau* on the table and started to walked away. I couldn't wait a moment longer.

"Missus?" I tried in English. "How much you pay?"

The lady returned and stretched the *pa'ndau* in front of her. "Um, thirty dollars?"

I hoped Americans bargained like the Thai traders. I knew I had to try. I waved my hand over the pile of storycloths and said, "Pretty . . . see?" I ran my fingers over the smooth stitches. "See? Good!"

"Yes, yes, I see. Very, very good. How much?"

This was it. I squeezed my chin as if I were thinking

hard. "Big one, forty dollar; little one, thirty dollar," I finally said.

The woman's face lit up, and she waved to ladies across the hall. "Come here! Look at these!"

Surprised, Grandma and I beamed at each other. More people hurried over, and before we knew it, we'd sold all the storycloths and two of the reverse-appliqué squares. I panted like a dog as I counted the money. Sixty dollars more than what I owed Grandma!

As I put the money in my pants pocket, I heard angry voices approaching. Grandma gripped my arm. The other Hmong ladies selling *pa'ndau* were rushing to our table. What was going on?

Uncle Ger stood in front of us, his arms wide to hold the women back. "My mother didn't know! It's their first time here. It's my fault. I didn't tell them the prices."

The man in the black suit reappeared and calmed the women. "Don't worry," he told them. "The fair goes on all weekend. We still have lots of time to sell your beautiful work."

Glaring at Grandma and me, the women slowly returned to their tables of unsold *pa'ndau*.

"What did we do?" Grandma asked Uncle Ger.

"I'm sorry. My fault," he said, pressing his fist to his chest. "We've been trying hard to raise the *pa'ndau* prices so that the women can get paid fairly for their long hours of work. You undercut their prices by half!" he finished with a wince.

I did the simple math in my head. I felt horrible for the other women. I almost felt worse for Grandma and me. We could have made over $500!

Grandma closed her eyes and swayed into Uncle Ger's arms. "We should go home," she moaned. "I can't keep my face in front of these women."

I didn't want to show my face to *anybody*. In only ten days I'd made two huge mistakes about money. No one had told me I'd need it so much in America.

Chapter 9

Back in the mountains of Laos there weren't many schools to begin with, and then the fighting closed most of them. Even in peacetime girls never went to school. Their mothers taught them how to cook, clean, sew, and care for babies. Girls worked in the fields, too. Boys rarely went to school either. Sometimes only the oldest son got to go. He would be sent to the city—usually Vientiane—and learn Lao and French, reading, writing, and math. Then he'd come home and teach other boys in the village. For most Hmong children the schools in the camps were their first and only schools.

Grandma had told me, "Hundreds of years ago, when we Hmong lived in China, we had our own alphabet. But the Chinese punished or killed us if they caught us using it. Over the years the alphabet was lost."

How could a whole people forget an alphabet? That makes the Hmong sound so dumb. We were not dumb. Grandma explained that the Hmong didn't do much that needed writing. "We farmed, we hunted, we made cloth, we cooked." The Hmong had children, who were forced to use the Chinese writing system. We forgot our letters.

When Grandma was younger, some missionaries made us a new alphabet. At first, mostly men learned it. Young men, not the old ones. Not too many girls got to learn it. After the war, in the camps, some girls like me were allowed to go to classes. I got to go because I didn't have little brothers or sisters to mind, and I was too young to get married. We learned to read Hmong, and we learned some Thai and English, all in the English alphabet.

This was the biggest surprise when I entered school in Providence: So many girls there! More girls than boys! Girls of all different skin colors. Lots of Hmong. I saw kids who looked Asian but weren't Hmong. Most of them were Cambodian, lowlanders from south of Laos, and Heather said they didn't get along too well with the Hmong. Some people had dark skin like Heather's boyfriend, Bobby. There were lots of Spanish-speaking people in every shade of tan. I wanted to be friends with everyone, but I was shy and scared.

On my first morning of school, I put on my new jeans, shoes, and shirt. Now that I had "earned" them, in a way, I felt proud to wear them.

I found Grandma on the couch in the living room. "Will you be fine alone, Grandma?" I asked. "What will you do all day?"

She pointed to the television Uncle Ger had brought us. I laughed to myself. Grandma wanted to watch TV, but she didn't want to touch it. The first time she had, a blue spark had flicked her finger. She was certain a bad spirit lived inside, but a spirit that made funny pictures and sounds to entertain her. So anytime she wanted to watch it after that, she made me turn it on for her. She probably wouldn't change the channel all day.

"Why don't you go visit friends or meet new ones at the market? You could do *pa'ndau* together," I suggested.

"Most of the women have jobs or look after babies. And after the problem at the fair, I don't want to face any of them."

I understood her shame. I was luckier. I hadn't seen any girls my age at the craft fair, girls I might face in school or in the neighborhood.

I kissed Grandma's cheek and said, "I'll wait for Miss Susan on the front steps."

Grandma pressed a bag of cooked rice into my hand and said, "Do well."

Of course I'd do well, I thought. To do anything else would shame my family. I wondered if Heather and Lisa did well at school. All they talked about was lunch! Heather acted like she didn't need school. But Lisa was harder to figure out. I decided she would try to please everyone and be a good Hmong girl.

Miss Susan's red car didn't seem so tiny with only two people in it. She asked, "How are you, Mai?"

Blinking uncontrollably, I couldn't remember the easy reply.

"That's okay—everyone is nervous on the first day. You'll do just fine." Miss Susan reached into the rear seat and pulled out a dark-blue pack. "Here. I bought this backpack for you to keep your things in."

"Thank you very much," I said, remembering the English now. When I took it, I could hear things knocking together inside. I unzipped the pack to find pencils, pens, notebooks, a ruler, and some other stuff. A fabulous aroma rose up, one I knew from PASS. I loved making that smell by rolling a pencil between my sweaty hands.

"All this is for me?" I asked in disbelief.

"Yes, of course, Mai."

Chills of gratefulness broke out all over me. "Thank you very, very much."

Miss Susan drove a short distance and pulled up in front of a huge brick building: Roger Williams Middle School. Providence certainly had a lot of things named after this Roger Williams. Later I learned that he was a refugee, but he didn't have to survive a war.

After Miss Susan showed me how to wear the backpack, we walked inside. The moment my foot hit the speckled floor, a loud ringing echoed in the halls. Louder than the smoke alarm in our apartment. I put my hands over my ears and ran back out.

Miss Susan came right after me. "Mai, it's okay," she said. "The bell is supposed to be loud, and you will hear it many times every day. It's a signal—a signal to tell students to go to a different room, or to see a different teacher, or to eat lunch."

Even after the bell stopped, the sound kept bouncing around in my head. But now the classroom doors had flown open. Kids spilled into the halls the way a river breaks through a dam. Their voices were louder than the bell! I tried to flatten myself against the wall, but my backpack stuck out. Kids bumped and nudged me—though not painfully. Here girls didn't have to walk behind boys. Many girls even went with boys, arm in arm or side by side, close like Heather and Bobby, Lisa and Lue. Touching, always touching. Hmong boys and girls, men and women, rarely touched. Even married people didn't touch a lot in front of other people. I wasn't sure if I'd ever get used to how much Americans touched each other. A little hug here, a pat on the back there, a kiss on the cheek, a handshake. You were expected to shake hands with someone you'd never even met before!

Every student and teacher passing me had a smell—some of orchid, some of ground coriander seed, some of camp refugees who hadn't washed in weeks. Ugh! Many of them were dressed in the kind of clothes my cousins had picked out for me. Quite a few had streaky choppy hair like Heather's, and some girls had hair so short, they looked like boys. In a flash, the halls emptied, as kids pushed themselves into the rooms. I was panting. What chaos!

"You'll get used to it," said Miss Susan as she squeezed my hand.

I would have to.

Miss Susan led me into an office and helped me fill out some papers. Then she led me down hallways that all looked the same. My new sneakers squeaked on the shiny floor, and my pink coat was reflected in the rows of silver lockers. The air smelled of metal and of the strong soap we'd used to clean the latrines in Phanat Nikhom.

Miss Susan pointed out the cafeteria.

"Ca-fuh-teer-ee-uh," I tried.

"Good!" she exclaimed. "That is where you will eat with your new friends."

The cafeteria sounded like a fun place. From all the kids I'd seen, I predicted that the food and water line would be very long.

"This is my class, L.E.P.," Miss Susan said, stopping and pointing to the letters on a wooden door.

"L.E.P.?" I repeated.

"L is for limited, E is for English, and P is for proficiency," she explained. I didn't quite understand. She spoke again, more slowly. "Some schools call it E.S.L.— English as a Second Language. You speak Hmong first, and you speak it at home. Others might speak Polish first or Spanish first."

I nodded. Miss Susan swung the door open, and all the kids stood and said in Hmong, "*Txais tos!* Welcome to Roger Williams!"

My eyes got very wet, and I covered my mouth to hide the quivering of my lips. For the first time since my arrival in America three weeks ago, I felt like I belonged.

Miss Susan introduced me to the other teacher, then showed me all the learning tools. At a place called the listening station, I tried on earphones. The words in my ears were also right in front of me in a book. Pictures showed a girl locked in a high tower. But she used her long, long hair—like mine but yellow—to help her escape with a prince. I had fun playing with the pretend kitchen and plastic foods. I'd done that in PASS in Phanat Nikhom, and it felt good to do something familiar. I paged through a big book that had many things for sale. Oi, I swore to myself, it would be a long time before I went shopping again!

At one table four students were playing a game. Miss Susan explained, "One person draws a picture, and the others guess what it is."

I watched a boy draw an egg and a pan. "Egg!" I said. I'd seen that word on the carton I bought at the store.

The boy laughed; then he pointed to the pan he had drawn. He motioned for me to follow him, but he didn't get up or move, and he didn't speak. I didn't understand what he wanted from me. More . . . more what?

One of the players, a Hmong girl with a heart-shaped face, leaned toward me and whispered into my ear. "*Fried egg.*"

"No fair, you're helping," the boy said, and laughed.

The Hmong girl rattled off some fast English, giggling the whole time.

"Mai, this is Yer, your student mentor," said Miss Susan. "She helps our new Hmong students."

"Hi!" Yer said, standing. She was my height.

In Hmong, I asked, "Are you like a teacher?"

"More like a friend. I'll help you find your way around, learn how to work your locker—you know, that kind of stuff. You'll be speaking English all the time with Miss Susan and other teachers and students. But sometimes your brain will want to shut down. So you can save up all your questions and ask me anything in Hmong."

I already had a question. "Will you be with me all the time?"

"If I were, you wouldn't learn a thing! And neither would I," she said. "No, you have to 'bathe yourself in English,' as the teachers say. I only come in here for an hour on Tuesdays and Thursdays. But we're both in the seventh grade, so we have the same lunch period. You can sit with me and my friends if you want."

Oh, I wouldn't be alone. How grateful I felt. Who was this girl who was so smart she could help the teacher? And she seemed so American—yet not in the same way as Heather and Lisa. For one thing, she had kept her Hmong name. Her hair looked normal Hmong, long and straight—no streaks or ratty edges. Yer dressed neater, in a kind of short sarong. And she was respectful and friendly, the way most Hmong would act.

I told her I would join her at lunch. She spoke in English to Miss Susan, then said to me, "It's all set. I'll meet you here at eleven-thirty, then we can walk to-gether. The cafeteria is so big, you might have trouble finding me if you go alone."

While most of the students came to L.E.P. and left after an hour or so, I spent the whole morning there, reviewing the alphabet and numbers. But the aromas from the nearby cafeteria made it impossible to concentrate. The smell of food never left the air. Americans ate all the time! Was that why so many of them were plump? When a bunch of kids went to lunch at eleven, passing our door on the way to the cafeteria, my stomach rumbled like thunder.

"It's hard, isn't it?" Miss Susan said, catching me with my eyes on the door. I lowered my head, ashamed I wasn't paying attention to the lesson. She patted my hand—that touching again—and added, "Many people new to America can't believe the food: how much there is of it, how good it smells and tastes. Refugees, more than other immigrants, hate how American kids waste food. Every American kid should spend a week in a refugee camp to see what real hunger is."

Had I understood her correctly? I was horrified that she would wish such a thing for children. But I soon discovered what she meant about the waste. As I followed Yer into the cafeteria that first day, I saw a boy dump half a tray of food into a trash can. I dug my hand in and saved half a hamburger and an apple with only one bite missing. An apple!

"Yer, how can people throw good food away?" I asked.

Yer spun and whispered, "Mai, drop that garbage. Drop it now. God, I hope no one saw you rooting in the garbage like a rat." She gave my hand a shake, and I sadly watched the food tumble back into the can.

"But"—my voice was shaky—"did you see that apple? I love apples!"

"Oh, Mai, I know, I know. I was like that at first too. But the American kids made fun of me. Called me bad names. A 'pig'!"

Bad names were nothing to me—I couldn't understand them anyway! Besides, I'd rather be a pig—a nice fat one—than ever starve again. That apple made me even more hungry, so when Yer turned her back, I took out my rice and gobbled it in two big pinches. When I put my empty bag in the trash, I could still see that shiny apple. I glanced around to make sure no one was looking. Quickly I grasped the apple and hid it in my brand-new backpack. Now I'd have two fabulous smells!

I followed Yer into a line that only took a few minutes—not a few hours as in Ban Vinai. Yer picked up a tray and slid it along a metal rail.

"Want pizza?" she asked.

"You mean I can have it?"

"Of course!"

Remembering our fun in the mall, I chuckled to myself. I did what Yer did and put a slice of plain pizza on my tray, then a bowl of green leaves, a small round cake, and juice. My mouth watered so much, I had to swallow three times. Then I saw Yer pull out some dollar bills and hand them to a lady in a gray uniform. I felt my lips quiver, and I was afraid I would cry like a baby. What was I thinking? I had no money to pay for all this food! And there was no Heather here to pull out twenty-dollar bills for shopping. No kind official offering $500.

"Come on, Mai," Yer said, motioning with her head.

"I can't—"

The lady in the uniform glared at me and punched some buttons. "C'mon, sweetie, the line is long," she growled.

I needed to put the food back, but too many kids were lined up right behind me with their own trays full. I had no appetite suddenly. I felt sick to my stomach.

Yer spoke in Hmong, "I signed for you already. You get free lunch. Didn't anyone tell you?"

I sniffled and tried to catch my breath. "No" came out in a hiccup.

She elbowed me forward. "Aw, it figures. It's really okay, Mai, believe me."

Yer sat with a bunch of Hmong girls and squeezed over to make room for me on the bench. She introduced her friends: Ka Chea, Millie, Lag, and Renée.

Ka Chea was thin like me, with thick hair that swept along her shoulders. "Yay! Now *I'm* not the most recent 'off the jet,'" she said, smiling.

Yer explained that Ka Chea had come to America just the year before. She had spent six years in Na Pho, a refugee camp east of Ban Vinai.

Lag was born in Ban Vinai but left soon after. Her family had tried living in France before coming to

America. I'd seen clothes like hers only in the show windows at the mall. She wore a lot of jewelry, too. I had heard of diamonds, but her ring was the first diamond I'd ever seen.

The sisters, Millie and Renée, wore clothes like the church gave Grandma and me. I was glad not to be the only poor refugee. Millie and Renée were the same age, but they didn't look anything alike. I wondered if they had one father and two different mothers. Most men didn't take more than one wife at a time in America. It was against the American law. But some Hmong still did, Heather had told me. And if they kept quiet, nobody bothered them.

We talked about Phanat Nikhom. Ka Chea remembered Miss Sayapong. "She is still the best teacher I've ever had. PASS was the only good thing about that camp."

I nodded, chewing the crunchy, tangy lettuce. I wanted to tell my new friends about the soldier, but I was ashamed. They might have thought I was bad, that I invited the soldier, that I deserved it. So I only said, "That camp was worse than Ban Vinai. And more dangerous."

Ka Chea and Lag nodded. Did they also know about what the soldiers tried with refugee girls? "The soldiers there are all slime," Ka Chea said.

"Slime?" I asked, repeating the strange English word. "What's slime?"

Ka Chea squished a pea with a spoon and pointed at

it. "That's slime. The slimy soldiers—three of them at once—made my big sister unclean. They damaged her so bad, she hanged herself because she knew no Hmong man would ever marry her."

A shiver went through my heart. I closed my eyes, but all I could see was the face of that soldier. When I opened my eyes, tears coated my lashes. And through that blur I saw Ka Chea's tears for her sister. I reached across the table for her hand, and she clutched mine. This new custom of touching felt wonderful.

Chapter 10

The most feared and respected animal in the land of the Hmong is the tiger. The tiger is always hungry. The tiger steals children, wives, chickens, and pigs. The tiger is clever and can disguise itself and trick us. Of course, I had never seen a real tiger, though I had made them real on my storycloths. On cloth they could not hurt me, could not claw or bite me. Tigers stayed away from refugee camps because the soldiers shot them. I also think that tigers stayed away because we Hmong had shrunk to skin and bones in the camps. The jungle offered juicier meals.

A week after I started school, Miss Susan took the L.E.P. class on a field trip to the Roger Williams Zoo. (Again this Roger Williams!) We rode in a small bus—bigger than a van but smaller than the buses in Thailand or the school buses here. Miss Susan pointed to things and had us repeat their names. "Fire hydrant . . . sidewalk . . . curb . . . traffic light . . . red . . . green . . . truck . . ."

The bus stopped inside a maze of roads, and we got off. Miss Susan called, "This way!" And the naming game went on. "Black bear . . . orangutan—what a funny word—peacock . . . tiger."

"Tiger!" I said in English, so loud that my classmates stared at me.

My heart pounded in fear, and I jumped back from the cage. A real tiger walked back and forth, back and forth, its head low, as if ready to pounce. Its eyes stared right through me. *Tsov tom!* How many times had I heard that warning: Tiger bite! But it had never made me turn to stone as I did in front of that cage. After a time I realized that Miss Susan was shaking me gently.

"It's okay," she kept saying. "We're safe with the tiger behind the bars."

She hustled me along to my classmates standing at the next exhibit. I allowed myself to be led the rest of the day. My mind remained with the tiger pacing, pacing, pacing in its cage.

More and more, Heather reminded me of that tiger. Her orange stripe had faded to brown, but she became like a caged animal. For one whole week she was not allowed outside her home except for school. Uncle Ger had smelled cigarette smoke on her breath, and he had slapped her and "grounded" her. One time that week I had to go downstairs earlier before dinner. When I walked in, Heather was pacing by the window. The window frame reminded me of the bars in the zoo.

"Heather, do you have an egg we could use?"

She didn't even face me. Her voice sounded like a

roar. "You know how to work the refrigerator by now, Mai. Get it yourself."

I felt shrunken as a piglet runt. I got the egg and left without another word.

But that Saturday Heather was let out, and she seemed happy again. She asked me to come with her and Lisa to Knight Memorial Library. "To study," Heather told Uncle Ger. She lifted a stack of books to prove it.

Even though it was early December, the low sun warmed us as we sat on the stone steps. Every time I opened my vocabulary book, Heather or Lisa would ask me a question. Or they commented about people walking or driving by. Was this how they studied?

"Mai, there!" Heather said, pointing. "See, *that's* a refugee. Check out those dorky pants."

I ran my hand down my jeans, feeling sorry for the poor kid. Had he no cousins to help him fit in? Really, all he needed was one pair of jeans. I wore mine every day, with a different top, and nobody said anything.

Soon Bobby and Lue drove up and hopped out of the car. Heather started speaking English with Bobby, and I couldn't follow everything they were saying. Lue and Lisa sat almost on top of each other and whispered. I opened my book again and pretended not to watch them talking close and kissing. Lisa and Lue had better be careful that Hmong people didn't see them, I thought. Word would get back to Uncle Ger, and he'd make them get married now.

"Oh, here comes Miss Brown-nose," Heather suddenly said in English. Loud enough for everyone to hear, too.

Brown-nose? I looked up from my book to see her motioning toward Yer. Heather snickered. "Brown-nose" must not be a good thing, because Yer ignored Heather as she passed. But she didn't ignore me.

"Hi, Mai," she said. "Coming inside?"

Heather's eyes shot over to me. I swallowed hard. I wanted to go inside. I'd never been inside the library, and I really needed to study. Plus I'd felt like an outsider since my cousins' boyfriends showed up.

But before I could answer, Heather replied, "No, Mai's hanging with us. In fact, we're going to go for a ride. Come on, Mai."

I stood shakily. I glanced from Yer to Heather and juggled my heavy books. Why were they making me choose? Finally, I begged, "Heather, I have math to do. I'd better stay and study."

Heather's eyes narrowed at me. After a moment she said, "Suit yourself."

Once Heather's back was turned, Lisa winked at me and said, "You know Heather. She'll get over it."

I hoped so.

I pushed through two sets of heavy double doors and was met by that pencil aroma a hundred times stronger. I inhaled deeply and gazed at all the shelves full of books. I felt smarter just being surrounded by them, as if their words simply floated into my head. People worked quietly at long shiny wooden tables with fancy green lamps. A section off this main room had rows of computers, like at the school library. I pictured myself at one, pressing all the right keys and—

"Your cousins are bad news," Yer hissed.

"What? I'm sorry."

"Heather and Lisa are bad influences on you," she whispered.

Well, they did do some bad things I didn't like to do—smoking, drinking, spending time alone with boys. But I couldn't say anything against my cousins, my own clan. What did Yer expect me to say?

We sat at a table and Yer leaned across it. "Mai, Heather goes out with a Puerto Rican!"

So *that* was Yer's problem? "Yer, Bobby is not so bad. Lue is Hmong, and he does worse things than Bobby, like drinking."

"Okay, okay, Mai. Since you think Heather is so great, I have to tell you."

I sat up straight and crossed my arms. This girl—who I thought was so smart and special—had so far told me nothing I didn't already know. Nothing could change the way I felt about my family. How could Yer pretend to be my friend in front of the teachers, then turn around and gossip about my family?

"Heather's *gangsta!*" she informed me.

"What's that supposed to mean? I don't know this word," I told her.

"Girls!" scolded a woman with a name tag, looming

over us at our table. "If you want to study, you may stay. But if you're here to socialize, please go outside."

I didn't get everything she said, but Yer smiled sweetly. "I'm sorry, ma'am." Then she dragged me into the bathroom. "Heather's a *laib!* She was mixed up with the gangs."

Heather had told me about the gangs. How when the Hmong first came to Providence, other kids picked on us, beat us up. Some Hmong started sticking together for protection and fighting back.

I argued with Yer. "What's so wrong about gangs? We Hmong have been fighting for freedom for thousands of ye—"

"Let me finish about Heather, Mai. Things got worse. Kids thought it was cool to be a *laib*—going against their parents all the time, skipping school, hurting others, stealing, selling drugs, *taking* drugs. And listen, Mai, not little bits of opium medicine. These new drugs kill people!"

Yer seemed like a truthful person, but maybe this story was one big fib. I hoped so. "And you have proof that Heather did these things?"

She nodded several times. "My neighbor is a lawyer who defends young criminals in court. He handled Heather's case," Yer said quietly. "She was arrested for possessing a small amount of crack—not enough to sell but enough to get high with. Many kids had to give the lawyer statements of truth, including me."

I slid to the cool tile floor and let everything sink in for a few minutes. Didn't Heather remember how horrible life used to be? All the violence we had escaped? How the camps themselves hadn't protected us from violence? Heather and Lisa had everything here in America. How could they risk losing it and breaking up our family? *Our* family. The family I was finally a part of.

I found my voice and asked, "Is Heather still 'gangsta'?"

"I don't think so," Yer said, joining me on the floor. "Lots of kids ended up in a special jail for young criminals. Heather was luckier and only had to do community service. A few years ago a group—the Indochinese Advocacy something-something—helped get rival gangs talking to each other, get them back in school. So most of the gangs are gone now."

"So then Heather is better?"

Yer hugged her knees. "I don't know, Mai. I hope so. But look—she still drinks and smokes, and, well, she's wild. Keep away from her, Mai, or she'll make you wild too."

After my talk with Yer, I threw myself into my studies. And when Heather and Lisa asked me to go out, I always told them no.

One night an hour after dinner, they got angry at me when I refused again. It wasn't even that they were going someplace special, like a movie or a party. All my cousins did was walk or drive around.

"Grandma is alone every day," I tried to explain in our doorway. "I need to do *pa'ndau* with her, and get her to practice speaking English."

"I thought my mom took her to the Genesis Center to make friends with people her own age and to learn English," Lisa said.

I closed the door behind me and stepped into the hall with them. "Grandma says the ladies we cheated at the craft fair are there, and she can't show her face."

Heather smirked. "The old people have such stupid ways." She said louder, and in English: "Get over it, Grandma!"

"Shh! Besides," I told them, "Grandma says, 'Why do I need to learn English when I have you to help me?' What am I supposed to say to that? 'No, you saved my life, but I don't have any time for you'?"

"Yes!" Heather said. "Say something exactly like that! She can't stop you anymore from doing what you want."

I lowered my eyes and sighed. Heather was right in a way. I now felt more powerful than Grandma. In only six weeks I had learned how to shop, how to take buses, how to use the telephone—which really scared Grandma. She couldn't figure out how voices squeezed through the lines. She thought that spirits put wings on the words. The truth was, I didn't need Grandma here. She needed me. And that's why I couldn't just leave her. It wasn't easy to be rude when I had been a good Hmong girl all my life.

"I can't go with you," I finally said. "Sorry."

"Ha!" Heather said. "*We* feel sorry for *you*—and your sorry life!"

"Heather!" Lisa scolded. "She didn't mean it, Mai. Daddy just got through lecturing her. She's only blowing off steam."

Off they went, and aside from our quiet dinners, I didn't see them again for two weeks.

Providence turned red and green during those days, since the Christian holiday of Christmas was coming. Uncle Ger and Aunt Pa Khu still believed in spirits and the power of ancestors, they said, but they also believed in a different, all-powerful God like Saub. Christmas celebrated the birth of this God's son on Earth. Next to the family altar of ancestors, Aunt Pa Khu set up a hut for this baby God, Jesus. She burned incense and offered food at both altars. That was a lot to keep up with.

Miss Susan had taught us all about American Christmas and gift giving, so Grandma and I had made little *pa'ndau* ornaments for everyone. I mailed a small storycloth of a plane flying over the ocean to Pa Nhia. On Christmas we gave Aunt Pa Khu an elephant like the one I had made Pa Nhia in the camp. Uncle Ger got a turtle, Heather got a heart, and Lisa got a cross-stitched star with dangling beads.

"We have gifts for you, too," said my aunt. "But dinner will get cold. Let's eat."

I watched nervously as Uncle Ger carved a huge turkey with a knife as long as his arm! I hoped he wasn't in the hair-cutting mood tonight. We all sat down together for dinner, but we ate as strangers. My cousins and I didn't say a word, and the grownups chatted about the weather and boring work. It was better than hollering, I supposed. Aunt Pa Khu had made mashed potatoes, and I kept my mouth full with three helpings.

After dinner my aunt and uncle gave Grandma a gleaming set of pots and pans. Heather and Lisa had chipped in with new cooking spoons and flippers and tongs and stuff. My aunt and uncle gave me a CD player with earphones. Such huge gifts! I felt strange, because our gifts to them were so lowly and handmade. But they knew we didn't have much money. We didn't have jobs or savings in a bank.

Heather tossed wrapped squares into my lap. "Merry Xmas," she said. I unwrapped two CDs—one heavy metal band, one rap, the same groups she listened to.

"Thanks," I said. I was happy to have a gift from Heather, even though I liked Hmong rock bands better. I had listened to them with Yer on her special earphones that let two people listen at once. Maybe now I could borrow a Hmong CD from her.

Lisa gave me two tops—a flowery shirt with a scooped neckline and a dark-green sweater with buttons all the way up the front. Lisa had a good memory. I had admired tops of hers like these.

"We're going to a Christmas party over on Broad Street," Heather whispered as her parents hung their ornament gifts on their pine tree. "Want to come?"

Broad Street! That was asking for trouble. The police were always stopping people on that street. Yer said there were special houses on Broad Street where everyone could buy drugs and take them right there.

"No thanks," I whispered. "It's too dangerous."

"No, it's not," Heather argued. "The party is at Bobby's cousin's house. They've got little kids there, and his cousin's band is going to play."

"And Mai," Lisa begged, "we've got no school for the next week. So don't tell us that you need to study. Come, please. You never do anything with us anymore."

True, I thought, feeling guilty. But my stomach had started to cramp. Probably from too much soda and potatoes.

"I'm sorry," I said. I wiped some sweat from my forehead. "I'd like to, but I don't feel so great."

"Yeah, right," Heather sneered, heading out. "Better get to bed early like a good little girl."

"Leave her alone," Lisa told her sister, but she looked hurt too. "Maybe we could do something together over the vacation. Go shopping?" She shrugged when I nodded. Then they left.

Wincing, I folded my arms over my stomach. Maybe it was the chocolate cookies on top of the soda on top of the turkey and potatoes. At last I told Grandma, "I don't feel good. I'm going up to bed."

Aunt Pa Khu stood and headed for the bathroom. "I have Alka-Seltzer. You probably ate and drank too much Christmas food."

Grandma took my elbow. "None of that American medicine. I have some mint leaves upstairs. I'll make Mai a tea. She'll be okay."

Now Uncle Ger stood. "American medicines work very well. No need for Mai to suffer."

Grandma's voice became sharp. "If it's bad again, I won't need pills for Mai. I'll need the shaman."

"Please," I moaned, "stop arguing. Just let me go to bed." Holding my stomach, I trudged upstairs. The twisting pain began to feel too familiar, like a nightmare that visits again and again. I hurried into our apartment, rushed to the bathroom, and closed the door.

How could this sickness follow me? How could it find me here in crowded America? It was supposed to stay behind with all the other pain, all the other ugliness, the screams, the gunfire, the faces of rapists. . . .

When I opened my eyes next, I was lying on my mattress. Light filtered softly through the shade. Tomorrow had already come. The new white strings on my wrist and the sweet incense in the air told me a shaman had come too. Had he needed to do *hu plig*—the soul calling?

Grandma's and Uncle Ger's voices cut through the haze.

"Your medicine was no good either!" Grandma said. "She still has a fever."

"The shaman's ways are outdated," Uncle Ger argued. "They're okay for sickness of the spirit, but not of the body. If this has been going on for years, as you say, we should put Mai in the hospital."

"No!" Grandma pleaded. "They'll cut her open. Her souls will flee!"

Then cut me open. Let my souls go and find my parents' souls. Yeah, cut me open.

131

Chapter 11

Darkness came and went. Light returned. Bright light. Bright round lights, bars of light, pinpoints of light in my eyes. Sounds too—beeps, pings, voices over loudspeakers. Heather and Lisa appeared at my bedside.

"Oh, Mai, we're so sorry," Lisa said. "We thought you were faking being sick because you didn't want to be with us. Is this the sickness you had in camp, too?"

I nodded. "Where am I?"

"The hospital!" Heather said. She sounded impressed.

I remembered the nervousness and fascination I had felt in the Phanat Nikhom clinic. I saw some of the same tubes and armbands. I suddenly wondered whether this doctor could send me back to Laos if I had a really bad disease.

I sat up, patting my stomach. Full of dread, I asked, "Did they cut the sickness out?"

"No," said Lisa. "A doctor told Grandma that the cure doesn't include surgery."

What exactly had they done? I did feel better. Mostly

I was thirsty. "Water?" I asked, my throat tight and sore.

Lisa gave me little chips of ice from a cup. "You're getting your water from that." She pointed to a bag of clear liquid. A tube ran from it into my arm.

When a nurse appeared, Heather said, "Mai wants to know what's the matter with her."

"Sorry, honey, I don't see your chart here" she said to me. "I do know that you're dehydrated—that you need lots of water. Doctor Patel will be here to talk to you soon."

As she left, Uncle Ger came in. "How do you feel, *maum?*" he asked.

"Tired," I said. "Where's Grandma? I want Grandma. What's going on?"

"Grandma didn't want to come inside. The doctors are doing some tests. They took blood from you and some samples of, uh, your *quav* and *zis.*"

"Did somebody order pissa?" Heather asked.

Lisa bent over, pretending to hold her stomach. "Gross!"

I smiled, too embarrassed and weak to enjoy the private joke very much. Uncle Ger shook his head.

Soon a lady doctor arrived and explained the test results: a parasite had made me sick. "We see many refugees with parasitic diseases. Yours is called threadworm."

This time both of my cousins bent over laughing, and even Uncle Ger smiled. What was funny? This disease, threadworm, was anything but funny to me. Dr. Patel looked confused too.

Uncle Ger told me in Hmong, and I had to giggle. To Dr. Patel he explained, "Our Mai and my mother are expert sewers of storycloths, *pa'ndau*."

"Oh, yes!" said the doctor. "I have a beautiful *pa'ndau* pillowcase."

Uncle Ger continued, "My daughters joke that the parasite came from the sewing threads."

"Ah." The doctor covered her mouth, but I could tell by her eyes that she was laughing too. Then she spoke seriously again. "In the camps the tiny worm probably entered through a cut in your foot, Mai. Or perhaps you ate rice with live threadworm eggs in it."

Heather gagged and gripped her throat. Lisa held her stomach. Uncle Ger scowled. All I could think of was that cute worm in my first apple. But I'd been sick way before that.

"Was it something the doctors in the camp could have fixed?" my uncle asked.

"Hmm. Perhaps for a short time. But the same unsanitary conditions that made Mai sick the first time probably made her sick again and again," Dr. Patel replied. She handed a small brown bottle to Uncle Ger. "The good news is that this medicine will cure it forever, because it's unlikely she'll pick up the infection here in America."

Uncle Ger grinned—in triumph, I think. I reached for the bottle and tried to read the label: "Thi-a-ben-da-zole. That's the biggest word I've ever said." Whatever it was, if I took it three times a day for a month, then I would never get the sickness again. And a *lady* doctor did it!

So much for Grandma and her old ways.

One evening, after I'd been home from the hospital for three days, Heather and Lisa came into our apartment, bundled in jackets and hats.

"We're going to First Night," Heather said. "We were wondering if you were strong enough to come with us."

I sat up on the couch. "What's First Night?"

Lisa's dark eyes brightened. "It's the American New Year. Tonight, December 31, is the last night of the old year. In downtown Providence there are rock bands, all kinds of food, and huge fireworks."

"And Daddy actually gave us some money to spend," Heather added. Lisa nodded when she saw my look of disbelief.

"New Year . . . I'd love to go. Can I, Grandma? I feel stronger."

Grandma didn't take her eyes from the old folks playing music on the TV. She didn't take her fingers from the appliqué triangles she was stitching. Not speaking a word, she nodded.

"Excellent!" Lisa said. "Put on lots of warm clothes and let's go!"

Right before we got to the bus stop, I felt a cool tingle on the tip of my nose. Then came another, on my cheek. In the light of the streetlamp I saw more drops—so white they were almost clear. Not clear like rain. Thicker, slower, and floating like tiny feathers.

"What is this?" I asked Lisa as I held out my mittens to catch some drops.

"Oh, you're such a refugee! It's snow! Snow! Our first snow of the year!"

"This is real snow?" I asked, happily confused. I'd seen "snow" on holiday displays, and it had looked perfectly real to me. The snow I'd seen in pictures and on TV looked smooth, and it covered everything like ash. And I had even stitched snow—little white dots of thread. But nothing had ever tingled on my skin this way. This had to be real snow.

"Mai's first snow. Wish I had a camera," Heather said. "We usually get snow way before Christmas. But it's been pretty warm lately."

"You call this warm?" I laughed. "Thailand is warm."

"Thailand is stinking hot!" Heather said. "All year long."

Lisa grabbed my arm. "Mai, stick your tongue out and catch one."

I tilted my head back and opened my mouth. Each snowflake fell with a tickle on my tongue. I opened my eyes and went chasing after as many flakes as I could.

"Watch out!" Lisa hollered. She yanked me back onto the sidewalk just as the bus screeched to a stop. "Whew! Listen, Mai, tonight, all night, you stay right next to us, okay? It's very crowded downtown. And sometimes it gets crazy. You could get lost or hurt."

"Yeah," Heather added. "Just stick with us."

On the crowded bus downtown we all had to stand. I studied Heather. Despite what Yer had told me, despite the mean way Heather acted sometimes, I had really missed my cousin these past few weeks. She was so daring. She had so much energy. I liked watching her. I never knew what she'd do next. Lisa was quieter, calmer. She acted protective, more like a big sister to me. Heather acted like . . . I didn't know. I'd never met anyone else like her. I didn't want to stay away from Heather, as Yer had warned me. I couldn't stay away. She was family. But . . . I had to know some things.

I gripped a hanging strap next to my cousin. "Heather?" I said, a bit shaky. "Did you ever take drugs?"

"What!" Heather shrieked. Passengers stared at us. "Where did that come from?"

I felt like disappearing. "Yer said—"

"Listen, Mai," Heather began, "I might not be a braino brown-nose like Yer and her friends. But I'm not that stupid."

"And you're not in a gang either?" I hoped aloud.

Heather switched hands on the strap so she could face me. "All you need to know is that Bobby and I are clean now, straight. We're fine, upstanding, law-abiding citizens. Just like you. Actually, you're still an alien—but a legal one!"

Lisa guffawed and elbowed me. "That was a joke."

I didn't get it, but my cousins' laughter made me relax a little. The noise on the bus grew higher and louder as we neared downtown. Everyone on the sidewalks was walking in the same direction. I'd never seen so many happy people in one place.

Once we got off the bus, I let Lisa and Heather lead me around and feed me, like a pet monkey. We ate spicy chili dogs—very messy—and warm pretzels that had pieces of salt the size of snowflakes. A man walking on stilts towered above the storefronts. A clown made a dog out of skinny balloons, and he presented it to me as if I were a queen. We passed by a stand where older Americans were playing the kind of music Grandma liked on TV. Then we stopped to watch a rap group. I couldn't understand what the singers were saying, but I liked the way they danced, lifting their knees high or sinking to a squat. But their underwear, showing above their jeans, made *me* feel embarrassed, though they didn't seem to care at all. The whole time, snow fell slowly, tingling my face and gathering on people's hats and shoulders.

I hollered to Lisa and Heather in Hmong, "It's wonderful to see so many people—not just Hmong—having fun together for New Year. I've never seen anything like this."

"You would have seen lots of things like this every year if Grandma had gotten your butts to America sooner!" Heather replied.

"*Raum,*" Lisa scolded, elbowing Heather.

I didn't really understand what Heather had said. Maybe I hadn't heard it right. "What do you mean, 'sooner'? Grandma and I came to America as soon as we were allowed."

"Heather, we're not supposed to tell," Lisa insisted.

Heather shoved Lisa's hand off her arm.

"Tell what?" I cried, shaking Heather's other arm.

Heather steered me into an alley away from the noise, Lisa hurrying behind us. "It's about time Mai knew," Heather stated. "It's too big a lie."

Lisa scowled. "Aren't you scared of what this will do to Mai?"

Heather took a deep breath and let it out. She and Lisa stepped away and whispered together. I felt stupid. Like a small child—people talking about me, right in front of me, as if I couldn't hear, couldn't possibly understand. My hands ached for something to do, something to hold on to. I broke a seam in my puffy coat and wound the thread tightly around my finger. I had a queasy feeling about what I might learn. Would Heather's words explain Grandma's moods this past year? Why she had been hiding inside herself like a snail in its shell?

I needed to hear what Heather had to say. "Tell me the truth," I insisted.

Heather's eyes met mine. She gave Lisa a little push away, then blurted, "You could have come to America when you were seven—at the same time we came."

My breath escaped in a steamy cloud. The corners of my mouth quivered, wanting to give way to wailing. But I wanted proof. "How do you know that?"

Heather and Lisa eyed each other; then Lisa sighed. "Heather's right. It's because your father was a secret soldier in Laos for the Americans, like our dad. That meant the U.S. government would let them and their families come to America whenever they were ready. Our parents used to talk about you and Grandma a lot when we first got here. My dad wrote lots of letters to Ban Vinai, asking the *naiban* to persuade Grandma to come. She wouldn't listen. Finally, word came that the camps were closing. Grandma had to choose between going back to Laos and coming here."

Tiger Mother, I swore, my eyes filling with angry tears. "I can't believe she didn't let me come. I can't believe that she lied to me for so long!"

Lisa touched my shoulder. "Try not to be too angry with Grandma."

"Not too angry?" Heather cried. "When *we* don't tell stuff, the grownups call it lying. When they do it, it's supposed to be fine? This lie has made me sick for years—especially since you came, Mai. It's way worse than any fib I could ever tell."

Fighting for control, I dried my eyes on my sleeve and nodded.

In a softer voice, Heather said, "Now can you see why I don't get along with Grandma? . . . It's best not to say anything to Grandma or Dad—you know, that we discussed this."

I pursed my lips, promising nothing.

Arm in arm, we made our way back to the First

Night celebration. Blossoms of light filled the sky. Screeches, whistles, and rumbles filled my ears, echoing a war I thought I had left behind. Now a new war was looming. Grandma had kept me in that stinking filthy camp for five extra years. *Five years!* She had kept me from the rest of my family. How could I *not* say anything to Grandma?

Chapter 12

"Why did you hold me back from coming to America?" I rehearsed in the bathroom mirror.

No, it was bigger than just America. And there was no "why," no good reason I would accept from her. I cleared my throat, narrowed my eyes, and tried again. "How could you hold me back from the only thing I ever asked for?"

But then Grandma could answer, "You asked for things all the time. I gave you those things. I gave you stories, rice, rubs on the back, blah blah blah . . ."

Try again. "How could you keep me from my family? What I wanted most in my life?"

And what if she said, "You had *me*. I was the only family that mattered. Certainly, these cousins are not what you wanted. Admit it."

One thing I had to admit: it was easier *not* to say anything to Grandma. Over and over again I vowed to confront her about her lie. But I didn't have the courage, and that made me feel ashamed. I behaved like the obedient Hmong girl I had always been. Serene, like the cold, quiet snow outside my window.

Doing *pa'ndau* together bored me now, frightened me too. If I'd spent any length of time with Grandma, the words would have spilled out, messy and uncontrollable. But *Why did you lie to me?* was easy and neat to ask—when I was alone. So I stayed in my room, avoiding her. "Studying," I told her every night. But the angry words didn't go away. They grew like weeds, taking over every inch of my mind and heart, until there was no room for any other thoughts or feelings. I practiced the conversation, trying out different faces in the mirror: pitying, offended, unbelieving. But every time, I ended up looking mournful, obedient, forgiving. Cowardly.

One evening Grandma put aside her *pa'ndau* and stopped me from going to my room. "Ger tells me I have to meet a welfare lady and maybe sign some papers tomorrow at an office. I need you to come with me again."

"I can't tomorrow," I said truthfully. "I have a math test."

Grandma put her hands on her hips. "My need for you is more important than any test. Take it some other time."

Before I knew what I was saying, I growled, "Why can't you go by yourself? Just take a bus. You're a grownup! You don't need me for every little thing."

Grandma slapped me across the face. "You show me respect! I have taken care of you since you were an infant."

My hand went to my hot face. Aside from rubbing off my lipstick, Grandma had never struck me in anger before. Now's the time, my brain shouted. The question. Ask it! "Why—"

"I'm sorry, sorry." She laid her hand softly on my stinging cheek and started to cry. "This is not like me, to raise a hand against you. I'm afraid that I need you too much."

She hugged me, but I could not hug her back. My arms stretched out on either side of her, as if they were wood. In a moment her shuddering stopped, and she walked away with her head down. "This is not like me to cry like a baby, either." She picked up a piece of paper from the living-room table and handed it to me. "This is where we must be at ten o'clock tomorrow morning. Do you know the street?"

I nodded. It was downtown. Not far from the spot where Heather had told me the news that had changed everything. I cleared my throat and muttered, "We'll leave here at nine-fifteen and catch the nine-thirty bus."

The next morning I walked to school a half hour early. At the office desk the secretary who never smiled sighed heavily at me. I asked to leave messages for my math teacher, my homeroom teacher, and Miss Susan. When I told the secretary what my message was, she said, "I'm afraid that is not an acceptable excuse."

I closed my eyes to calm myself and think of the right American words for this mean lady. "My uncle, he works. My aunt, she works. My grandmother—has no English. She cannot read."

The secretary wrote the messages and stuck them in

the teachers' mailboxes. "Your math teacher is very strict and may fail you anyway. It would be easy for you to get the answers from a friend."

My throat became tight, and I was afraid I'd cry from shame right there. I rushed out and down the steps so fast, I slipped on ice and hurt my elbow when I landed. Little chunks of salt stuck to me, and a chalk-skinned boy laughed. "You chinks don't know nothing about the cold weather, do you? Why don't you go back to where you came from?"

The tears came then, and I wiped them away real fast. Kids would be coming to school. I needed to be done with it. Besides, I could let Grandma see my anger but not my pain. I would not give that to her.

At the welfare office an official named Ms. Goodrow led us through a maze to a tiny office. She wore a brown skirt-and-jacket suit, and her skin was brown like Bobby's. She asked in a friendly voice, "And how are we today?"

I translated for Grandma, who had already taken out a *pa'ndau* section half filled with elephant footprints—symbolizing wealth. Grandma replied, "Tell the dark lady I'm always too cold, and everyone's so busy that nobody pays attention to me, and everything is plastic and too fast. . . ."

I don't think Ms. Goodrow expected Grandma to answer for real! She tucked in her chin and leaned back.

"My grandmother is fine," I told her.

"Oh," she said, more businesslike. She flipped through some files and pulled out a thin one that had our names on it. "You have been here for ninety days. And you've been in school for almost as long, I see. Has your grandmother tried any of the job-training sessions or language sessions at the Genesis Center?"

I knew the answer and started to speak, but Grandma nudged me for the translation. Then she replied, "I am an old lady. I cannot work anymore, except with my threads and needles. What does she want me to do? It's so cold here. I can't remember any words. When is it going to get warm?"

I did all I could not to roll my eyes the way Heather always did. Ms. Goodrow raised her brows to me, expecting an answer. "No about job training, and no about language," I answered.

The official paged through our flimsy file and muttered, "I don't see any men of working age in this household." I shrugged. "So there is no income?"

"In... come?" I asked.

"No money coming in," she clarified slowly. "If no one can work, there is no money other than what the state is giving you. Correct?"

Uncle Ger's face flashed in my mind. Although he and Aunt Pa Khu and the church helped us and fed us, they hadn't given us any money. My aunt and uncle barely had enough for themselves, Heather had told me.

Grandma nudged me again, but I waved her off. "No money," I replied.

Ms. Goodrow took out a clean form and began filling it in with information from our file. "Please have your grandmother sign her name here. This will increase your monthly payment a little."

I reported this good news to Grandma. Grandma started blabbing, "No, no. Tell the dark lady we can't take any more money we don't work for. My son will take care of us."

Was she going insane? Uncle Ger and Aunt Pa Khu worked long hours, and they couldn't even buy a house. I took a deep breath and said, "My grandmother says I sign. She is . . . embarrassed? She can't write her own name."

Ms. Goodrow nodded knowingly and put her initials next to my signature. "And how are the food stamps working? Are you getting enough to eat?"

I pictured the American grocery store and the nearly empty cart we rolled up and down the aisles. Grandma gave Uncle Ger two hundred dollars of our stamps since we ate dinner at his table, leaving only fifty dollars a month for us. There was so much I wanted to try— sweet cereals I'd seen on television, cookies and fruit drinks kids brought in their lunch bags, snacks of pizza I could take right out of the freezer and cook in the oven. My mouth was beginning to water. Did I dare to ask for more?

"My grandmother does not eat well. She thinks the food will . . . go away. If we could buy a little more . . . ?"

Ms. Goodrow filled out another form for food stamps

right there and then. Fifty dollars more! I couldn't believe I had gotten her to do that. It was so easy.

As she ushered us toward the door, she gave me a small card. "Call me if you have any problems—especially with heat. The landlords can get awful stingy in the winter."

I had no idea what she was talking about, but she had said "heat." I told myself to ask her about that next time. I didn't want to ask for too much at once.

On the way home Grandma was acting like a world traveler. "I told you I needed you. Everything worked out fine."

She didn't know *how* fine, and I wasn't going to tell her. I just hoped I'd have this good luck with my math teacher.

When I told Miss Susan about missing my test, she said, "Don't worry. This kind of thing happens once in a while with new Hmong—actually, any new immigrants. The children learn English faster than their parents and grandparents."

Miss Susan always understood everything. I bet Miss Sayapong was that way too. I just hadn't gotten to know her as well. I wondered how a person could listen so completely, as if I'd spoken directly into her ear. Miss Susan saw with *my* eyes, felt with *my* heart. And as she replied to my questions, it felt as if the answers had always been inside me.

"I will talk with your math teacher and get the test," she said. "You can take it in my class. That way if you have any questions, you can ask Yer."

"But Grandma will probably need my help again and again."

"Yes, but here is how you *can* help. Try to make appointments for Saturday mornings. Many aid offices are open on Saturdays. And next time you go to the school office, speak to the secretary who's, um, the heavy woman. She's very nice."

The more I took Grandma out into the world, the more I got to translate, and the more I expressed *my* needs rather than Grandma's, the better we ended up. Chills of daring ran through me when I could make Grandma and an officer or clerk believe me. This thrill was what Heather must live on, I realized.

Uncle Ger had convinced Grandma to use more American colors in her *pa'ndau,* so he could more easily sell some at his factory. One day he gave me money for *pa'ndau* supplies—four ten-dollar bills and two five-dollar bills—fifty dollars! So on Sunday Grandma and I took a bus to a big fabric store near the mall.

At first Grandma's mouth dropped open at the size of the place. Big as an airport! The ceiling lights bounced in our eyes. We walked up and down the wide aisles of bolts of cloth, pillow stuffing, buttons, trims, needles, thread and yarn, and scissors. Everything we could possibly want.

Yet in a short while Grandma's eyes grew dull. "Everything looks the same," she muttered. "Everything is made by a machine. Like in the big grocery store."

I agreed with her. Hand-woven Hmong cloth was rich and sturdy. Some of the cloth here looked as flimsy as paper. But machines also made sewing easier. When I did *pa'ndau,* I longed for a machine to do the tedious parts—the trims and borders and hems.

I grabbed some yarn and said, "This looks like it was spun the old way."

Grandma brought the bright-orange skein to her nose. She rubbed a strand between her fingers. "This is made by a machine. It is the same material as a plastic bag."

Grandma wouldn't be happy with spun gold! I tossed the yarn back into the bin.

"Ger said get red, white, and blue material and threads," Grandma ordered. When I fetched her a bunch of bolts, she complained. "What am I to do with this red? It's the shade of blood when it first breaks through the skin."

"Americans like the colors of their flag," I explained.

"And this green cotton? It looks like the floor of the airports."

"Americans like to fly places," I said, getting impatient. I happened to like that dark shade of green. It would make nice curtains, like the ones I saw in Yer's front window. I grabbed a long roll of the material and heaved it into our shopping cart.

As I was struggling to fit the last bolt of fabric into our cart, a worker in a blue apron came over. "May I help you bring this to the cutting table?"

"What . . . table?"

The lady made her fingers into a scissors and pretended to cut my material. Then she coaxed us around the aisle to a counter. She rolled out the white bolt she was carrying for us and asked, "How much material do you want?"

When I translated the question, Grandma held her arms out wide.

The lady measured out the cloth and asked, "Like this? Two yards?"

"How much money?" I asked her, and she pointed to a label on the cardboard part of the roll: "$2.89/yd." That must have been the word she used, "yard." Only $2.89? I checked the other colors. Blue was the same price, and red and green were both on "Winter Sale" at $1.99. I did the math quickly and realized I might just get my curtains!

Grandma inspected the cut white cloth and nodded. "Get twice that of the other colors," she ordered.

"Look, Grandma, over there is silk embroidery floss. Why don't you choose some?"

"I don't want to go alone."

"Grandma, I can see you from here, and you can see me. If you get the floss, while I wait for the cloth, we'll finish faster."

"Faster, faster," she muttered. She raised her voice to sound like mine and added, "Americans like faster faster."

When she reached the display, she turned around and gave me a little wave, as if she were a three-year-old testing how far she could stray. I put on a smile and waved back.

Before she could return, I placed the green bolt on the table and asked for eight yards. I then ordered four of both red and blue. I folded the green immediately and placed the other cut cloths over it. The worker handed me a list with the prices. We still had plenty of money.

I thought about the way Americans figured out what something cost. I disliked it for many reasons. It was hard to know the price of something when there wasn't a number or sign on it. These bolts had prices, but sometimes all you saw were those little black bars on the back of the merchandise. The machine that read the bars looked like a gun. Or the clerk ran the bars over a dark piece of glass. Were there special eyes under the glass? Did they ever make mistakes? Ah, mistakes, I thought.

When the cashier entered the prices of our cloth and thread, our total came to $53.63. I caught my breath. Was I wrong about money again? Then more buttons were punched, and the total came out as $42.90.

The cashier must have noticed my confusion. She pointed to a blood-red sign saying "Super Markdown! 20% off everything in the store." I didn't understand the whole thing. All I knew was that I had handed her all my bills, and she gave me back my own $5, plus two $1 bills and ten cents.

At home Grandma immediately measured out and cut the materials. When she picked up the green material, much more unfolded. "Mai, the green should be the same size as the blue and red. Did you buy more?"

I knew Grandma would ask about the extra, and I had planned my response on the bus ride home. "Oh, I forgot to tell you. The woman who cut the cloth made a mistake. She said I could keep it, because now she couldn't sell it to anyone else."

"It didn't cost us more?"

I shook my head fast, feeling bold again. "I'll take the extra. I can use it to make curtains for my room."

I kept the extra money, too, on the top shelf of my closet. Uncle Ger never did ask for the change, so I didn't have to actually fib to him. A month later I used some to buy myself a treat—some chocolate cups with peanut butter inside. I ate them at my window seat, with the curtains wrapping around me like the silky inner husks of corn.

Chapter 13

Dear Mai,

Thank you for your letters and for the airplane storycloth. I am sorry I haven't written. I am very busy. I am now the third wife of Xiong Bee. The old wives work the corn with Bee, and I must watch all their children. Eight of them! And Mai, I am to have a child very soon. Maybe by the time you read this. I have to cook all the food, too. I am told I can rest a little when the baby comes. But not for long. The other wives would call me lazy. They work hard. The soil the Lao Communists gave us is very poor. The Westerners helped us build a well, but the water is so bad, we must boil it before we drink or cook with it. I'm exhausted.

I remember how we loved school at Ban Vinai. I have not seen a book since we moved here. Can you go to school in America? You were always smart. Do you still do pa'ndau? Pa'ndau, farming, marriage, and babies is the only way to live here. And making a baby hurts. Mai, don't make a baby for a long, long time. The first wife says it doesn't hurt when you're older. I don't want to make any more babies. But I have no choice.

I must stop now. Bee forbids me to write. He lets me read your letters, but he rips them up so I don't dwell on your good fortune. But please keep writing. Your letters are worth the beating. Your letters are my only dreams. Goodbye, friend.

I pressed Pa Nhia's letter to my heart and fell, crying, onto my bed. I pictured her with a big round belly, wiping children's noses and cleaning up their messes. I saw how tired she was. Pa Nhia, the champ at volleyball. Pa Nhia, who could not work with numbers so well. Oh, Pa Nhia—

A hand on my back startled me and I sat up. As I dried my tears, Grandma said, "What is the news from our homeland?"

I told her about Pa Nhia's situation.

Grandma gazed out my window—all the way to Laos, it seemed. "It doesn't sound so bad. It's better than being here with all the roads instead of paths. The streets have lamps so bright, I cannot see the stars. And there's no place to plant anything."

I wanted to push her out that window and say, "Go back there, then!" But I calmed my breathing and said, "I like it here, where I can go to school and not have babies all the time."

Grandma turned from the window and ran her finger along the sill. Examining the dust on her finger, she asked, "Mai, do you remember Yia from Phanat Nikhom?"

I remembered him all the way from Ban Vinai! From

the bus. From Phanat Nikhom. How could I forget him and his gentle ways? And Koufing, the little boy. I nodded.

"If I had said yes to Yia, he would have married you and you would make babies and have no school too, like Pa Nhia."

Another secret! Yia had actually asked for me? My thoughts and feelings clashed, and I dived into my mattress. Pictures flashed like a film inside my closed eyes. Yia's sweet smile, Pa Nhia's lovely handwriting, the satin of Koufing's straight dark hair, the dolls Pa Nhia and I made out of *pa'ndau* scraps, Pa Nhia's round belly, my round belly, chasing Koufing with my belly round and heavy, Yia gone all day to work, no books for Pa Nhia, no books for me.

Grandma had told Yia no. How had he reacted? It didn't matter. He had wanted me in his family. Grandma had brought me to my own family. I was glad she had done that. Yet it had taken her *five years!*

Grandma left, my door closing with a soft click. It also shut the room in my mind where I had kept all the pictures of Yia. In the five months since I'd seen him last, he was sure to have taken a wife in Massachusetts. How stupid of me to care. I had what I wanted right in front of me. Taking a deep breath, I got up, fished around in my backpack, and began my vocabulary homework.

A special church holy day called Easter was approaching, Aunt Pa Khu explained. She and Uncle Ger were going to church almost every night, and that Friday there was no real dinner prepared.

"Oh, I'm so sorry," Aunt Pa Khu said, putting bowls of cold fish and vegetables on the table for Grandma and me. "Today we don't eat much—no meat. It's a very solemn day, the anniversary of when Jesus—the son of our God—died." She nodded toward a portrait of a bearded man with his heart out of his chest.

How horrible. That must have hurt!

"But this Sunday we celebrate, because Jesus came back to life," Uncle Ger explained.

Maybe that's why Jesus's eyes are still open in the picture, I thought.

"Sunday is a joyous day in church," said Lisa. "It would be the perfect time for you to learn more about our God. Would you like to come with us? The church will be full of happy prayerful people. Hundreds."

While chewing a pickled egg, I raised my eyes toward Grandma.

She replied directly to her son. "I have told you several times in the past few months, we have no use for a different god, solemn days, joyous days, exchanging money, running back and forth to this 'church.'"

I had to admit, worshiping together with so many people sounded strange. I liked the quiet of calling on our ancestors, the flicker of the candle on the wall.

"Church this, church that," Grandma continued. She spat the word as if it tasted rotten. Why did she think that badly of the church—because she was embarrassed in their basement hall? It was the church that had given us clothes and food for free. Maybe going there with my family would be a way for me to thank them. Grandma might stay home and close her mind to different ways to worship. But I had lots of space open for new ideas. When it came to gods and spirits, I needed all the help I could get!

I turned to my cousins and asked, "Are you both going on Sunday?"

Lisa nodded. Heather nodded and added a roll of the eyes.

"Okay, then I'll go too."

"Good!" said Uncle Ger, with triumph in his voice.

Grandma pushed away from the table and stomped upstairs.

On Sunday morning Aunt Pa Khu wore a flowery dress and high heels. She had found an old yellow dress of Heather's for me to wear. I stuffed tissues into the toes of Heather's clunky black shoes and tried to walk without falling. Even Lisa and Heather dressed fancy. Heather wore her only other dress—a black one that fit closely to her body.

I had never gone in the front entrance of St. Michael's Church. It looked like a castle, with a statue of a winged man guarding it. At the door Uncle Ger told me, "The church is very good to the Hmong. We have our New Year downstairs in the hall too."

I followed my family inside. They dipped their fingertips into a bowl of water and touched their forehead, their chest, then each shoulder. I did the same. Oi. The bottom of the bowl was slimy, and the water dripped down between my eyes.

We walked into the main part of the building and a warm, spicy smell—like the shaman's incense—hit me. But nothing else looked like the shaman's altar. Stretching up to the ceiling, colorful windows showed pale-skinned people in long robes. Pots of white lilies decorated a stone table in the front. Long benches held people of all colors—including a lot of Hmong. Yer was there! With all seven kids, her family took up a whole row. And Miss Susan sat two rows up from them.

The moment I sat, a loud sound reverberated all around me and right up through the wooden benches into my body. I clutched Lisa's arm. She grinned and pointed up behind us. A woman in the balcony was playing a pianolike instrument I'd seen on *Sesame Street*.

"It's called an organ," Heather said, winking at Lisa for some reason.

Lisa giggled, then asked me, "Do you like the music?"

I shook my head and folded my hands in my lap to calm the jumpiness. I couldn't stand the way my bones vibrated. No Hmong instrument affected me that way.

Before the ceremony started, Aunt Pa Khu explained that Jesus had come back to life to show us the way to Heaven, to an Ancestral Kingdom. Soon we stood for a procession of robed men, women, and older children coming down the aisle. They got to sit on the platform in the front. Then after the music ended, we sat, and the talking began. The priest spoke so fast, I couldn't translate for myself. And the songs sounded nothing like the American music we listened to in PASS, nothing like Hmong chants, either. People seemed to follow along with books. I couldn't find the spots, but it was good reading practice. We stood and sat and stood and knelt and sat and stood again. Church was more like gym class!

Walking home, I asked, "Were those Hmong songs and chants to the spirits, just translated into English?"

"No." Lisa linked my arm in hers. "Mai, do you realize that people all over the world believe different things, sing different songs, and pray to different gods? Look across the street. That's a church."

"It's a store," I said.

"Read the window sign. They've got a cross, too."

I shook my head, confused. "So what's different about your beliefs now?"

"In our new religion our God is like Saub. And the church's saints—special ancestors—are kind of like our spirits. But in our church we don't believe that rocks and trees have spirits. Or that when you are reborn, you become another person."

I walked silently for a while. The only sound came from the crushed Pepsi can Heather was kicking. It made me think of recycling—how Americans make new things from old things. That was sort of like reincarnation, wasn't it?

"Well, if you don't become other people or things after you die," I asked, "what can a person hope to become?"

"That's the best part," Uncle Ger answered. "Our souls go to live with God in Heaven. We are reunited with our loved ones and live in eternal peace and happiness."

I kept walking, thinking of my parents. I had always feared that their spirits wouldn't be happy because their bodies had not been buried properly, if buried at all. We didn't get a chance to choose the day and hour of their burial. They weren't ready—weren't wearing *pa'ndau* and shoes of hemp. They probably were wearing metal, too, which might bring misfortune to those left behind. (Maybe that was why Grandma and I had suffered so much!) Grandma had told me that my father always kept his gun beside him and his bullets on his belt when he slept in the village. And no animals were sacrificed for my parents. You could not call the pigs and chickens killed by the poison gas proper sacrifices. Most important, no one had released my mother's and father's souls. For all Grandma knew, we were the only ones who had survived in our small village, and we had left too quickly to perform this duty.

I prayed now—to whom I didn't quite know—that our burial customs did not matter to this God. I asked that the souls of my parents had reached this new Heaven, that they were not wandering, dispersed and angry, never becoming whole again. The prayer left me with a strange feeling, a lightness, as if I had been carrying around all the metal in this world until now.

That afternoon my aunt and uncle gave a big feast. Uncle Ger had more beers than I'd ever seen Heather or Lisa drink together. And for a moment everyone acted happy. No scissors threatened, no silences, no arguments.

After we cleared the dishes, Aunt Pa Khu gave me a colorful basket of candy. I recognized chocolate-covered peanut butter eggs and swooned. There were jelly beans and marshmallow chicks and a coconut-filled bunny. She also gave me a cross made out of chocolate. Wasn't the holy man in church nailed to a cross? I was supposed to eat this holy symbol?

Grandma grabbed for my cross, but I pulled it away. "This may be your home, Ger, and your new beliefs. But that will not come into *my* home," she ordered. "It will insult our ancestors to bring it near our family altar."

"Mother, calm down," Uncle Ger said with an easy smile. "It is just some candy."

I unwrapped the cross and breathed in the rich chocolate aroma. Even though I had eaten three egg rolls, plus steamed vegetables, I wanted to gobble up the cross. Maybe it would make me holy too!

"In my home Mai will obey me," Grandma insisted.

Heather whispered to me in English, "A battle for Mai's soul. Who will win?"

"Me," I replied under my breath. I chomped into the cross and bit off the whole top.

Grandma's eyes grew as big as the colored eggs in the table's centerpiece.

Drooling, I managed to say, "You said the cross shouldn't come into our home! So I will finish it here!"

Grandma was the only one who didn't laugh.

One warm spring day in Miss Susan's class, Yer said, "Mai, a bunch of us formed a dance troupe and we perform a few times a year. We're going to dance in costume for the school's cultural arts fair next month. Do you want to come to our practice after school at my house today?"

Dance? I had never danced. But it wasn't often that someone besides my cousins invited me anywhere. I couldn't say no, or she'd never ask again. "Okay," I replied.

After school I finished my homework quickly and asked Grandma's permission to go to Yer's.

"No, you might get in the shopping habit again," she said, not taking her eyes from the cartoon on TV.

I picked up a length of scrap embroidery floss off the floor and twisted it around my finger. I thought I'd go crazy if I had to listen to these dumb voices on the TV all afternoon. What could I make up to convince her? Wait. Maybe the truth . . .

"Grandma, I'm going to watch Yer and her friends practice a Hmong dance they're going to do at a school fair."

Now she looked at me. "Can I see this dance at the fair?" she asked.

"Yes, I guess," I replied. "I'll find out the details."

"You may go to Yer's house, but be back before it gets dark."

Wow, that had been easier than I thought. "Yer and her friends sound very nice," she went on. "Not like Heather and Lisa, who don't respect anything Hmong. Would you like to invite Yer over here sometime? I would like to meet her."

Surprised, I tilted my head at Grandma. Ever since the pa'ndau sale disaster, she had been shy and scared to meet anyone. Now she wanted to have guests?

"That would be fun," I admitted. "We'll have more time when school lets out. I'll ask her then."

At Yer's house about ten girls had gathered in the grassy backyard. Along the rear fence grew shoots of different plants. I recognized peppers and cilantro. The garden gave me an idea. We couldn't plant things in the yard behind our house—it belonged to somebody else. But we could grow things in pots. I'd seen pots overflowing with flowers, hanging from people's porches or sitting on the rear fire escapes. Yer's back steps had such pots. It must be an American tradition, I decided. A good one.

"Attention!" Yer called, clapping. "The rehearsals for the fair have officially begun. And Mai will be dancing with us for the first time."

"Me?" I asked, terrified.

"Excuse me, but is there anyone else by the name of Mai here this afternoon?" The girls giggled as Yer pretended to survey the yard. "No, I don't see any other Mais."

"But I don't know any of the dances," I protested. "And I've never done any."

Ka Chea pulled me out of my chair. "We'll teach you, knucklehead!"

"Knucklehead?" I repeated, acting offended. I had no idea what a knucklehead was, but it hadn't sounded too bad coming from Ka Chea.

"Pop the music in, Yer," Ka Chea said, "and let's choose a few songs."

Yer had a selection of Hmong traditional songs and a few CDs by Hmong rock groups. We decided on one of each.

"Can I see what you've done before, so I know what it's like?" I asked, fiddling with thread in my pocket. I remembered a bit of dancing at New Year in Ban Vinai, but we didn't have much music in camp. It's hard to dance with no music.

Yer rummaged through more tapes and CDs, then started a new cassette. The girls lined up and danced separately, but they all did the same moves, sort of like the Hawaiian girls I'd seen on TV. Hips swaying—but slowly—and hands waving shapes in the air. It looked like fun, but I could never do it in front of hundreds of people!

I continued watching as they created movements to the new songs. Ka Chea always offered complicated arm and hand positions. She danced as if she had been born dancing. Yer and Lag made Ka Chea's moves simpler for everyone else. After a while they pulled me into their lines and taught me the steps. When the music began, I tried to follow, but I kept turning the wrong way or forgetting the correct movement. Once my hand flew wildly, and I smacked Ka Chea on her backside.

"Oi!" she screeched. She growled and chased me around the backyard. The girls caught me and, giggling, held me still. Ka Chea wound up and smacked my bottom so hard it stung through my jeans, but I couldn't stop laughing.

"See?" I squealed. "I told you I can't dance. I'm as graceful as a donkey!"

Getting back in line, Lag said, "I think Mai is going to need more time to, um, become more graceful. And we only have a month until the fair."

"Thank you," I said to Lag. "I have to go home now anyway."

"You won't get off that easy!" Ka Chea yelled.

Yer added, "We dance at New Year, too!"

New Year? I'd forgotten about New Year. It was only five months away! I bounced all the way home, picturing myself dressed up in *pa'ndau* and celebrating with my new friends and family. Then I remembered that Heather and Lisa didn't even go. And I wondered if I would still be mad at Grandma then. We were supposed to throw away all debts, all grudges and sadness, and make room for good things to come. Where would I find the courage to speak with her before New Year?

Chapter 14

The cultural arts fair took place a week before school ended. I brought Grandma to Roger Williams Middle School early so I could show her my classrooms, the cafeteria, and my locker. When we came to Miss Susan's door, my teacher was packing away games until September. I'd be meeting with Miss Susan this summer at the library, where she'd tutor me in American history. I needed to catch up to the students in eighth grade.

"So good to see you!" Miss Susan said, extending her hand.

"Shake her hand," I instructed Grandma in Hmong. Grandma obeyed.

Miss Susan pointed to the wall with our stories on it. "Mai writes beautifully. She has an excellent English vocabulary, though she does need work on spelling and grammar—a lot of work!"

I blushed, then translated for Grandma, "Miss Susan says I have lots of good English words, but I don't put them together so well."

"Sometimes when you're with Heather and Lisa, you

don't put *Hmong* words together so well," Grandma said.

I frowned, and Miss Susan asked, "What did she say?"

"Uh, uh, I got my talent for words from her."

Miss Susan laughed.

Grandma's eyes ranged along the walls, bright with pictures and English words. I realized she couldn't find my retelling of "Saub and His Fire," so I guided her over to my composition and illustration. I explained in Hmong that we had to put a folktale in our own words.

She nodded, pretending to closely inspect the swirls and lines of my penmanship. Smiling slightly, she faced Miss Susan and said, "This is why I need her so much. Her English is very good."

Miss Susan raised her eyebrows, expecting a translation. Part of me felt ashamed of how I'd been translating for Grandma—deliberately changing words and meanings, leaving out important things, and putting in little fibs. I could never tell Miss Susan how I *mis*used my English. But still, I stammered, "Grandma says I have the very best teacher."

Now it was Miss Susan's turn to blush. I was glad I could please her.

Miss Susan accompanied us to the auditorium. Grandma insisted on sitting in the front row, and I sat between her and Miss Susan. I had to tell Grandma eight times that it wasn't time for the Hmong dance yet. She didn't care about the Polish music, the Irish step dancing, and the other acts that came earlier in the program. I found them fascinating. I wanted to go to every country in the world.

"Finally!" I said, pointing to the program. "Yer's group."

We heard their jingling first, the silver coins and trinkets decorating their traditional *pa'ndau* costumes. The crowd said, "Ohh," when the girls took the stage, and the people applauded before the music even started. Grandma's smile widened into a crescent moon. I hadn't seen that smile since the very first day we'd arrived. I felt shame again. In the past seven months I had done little to make my grandmother smile. But then I thought, if she had brought me to America sooner, I'd probably be up there on the stage myself!

Ka Chea and Yer danced in the front row. They were the best and didn't make a single mistake. At one point Lag spun a few notes too soon, but nobody in the audience seemed to notice or care. No one pointed or jeered. And Lag just giggled before picking up the routine again. I started imagining myself in line with the girls, all dressed up and jingling in time to our whispery and flutey music. Maybe I could be good enough by October, for New Year.

After the show Miss Susan, Grandma, and I strolled to the cafeteria for refreshments. We picked up lemonade and, yum, peanut butter cookies. Yer's whole family was there—aunts and uncles and grandparents. And Ka Chea with her family, and Millie and Renée with theirs. The Hmong had taken over the caf! And I wanted to meet everyone.

When I turned to introduce Grandma, I found that she hadn't followed me over to Yer's group. Where was she?

I checked the bathroom first. There was Grandma, all alone, facing the mirror, her fingers barely touching her cheeks. Mirrors weren't new to her, but I'd never seen her linger in front of one before. What was she looking at? I didn't know what to say.

A toilet flushed suddenly, and we both jumped. I didn't want any of my friends to see Grandma upset, so I led her out to the hall and back into the auditorium, now empty and dim. She sat in a seat and faced the stage. Finally, she spoke.

"The dance was so beautiful, I almost cried. I haven't seen such costumes and dancing in years. There was some at Ban Vinai, but not so joyful as this. And the people—Americans, sitting right in these seats—loved it!"

"Then why are you upset? This is a happy time."

"I followed you into the eating place, and a little toward Yer's family. But two women there pointed at me and whispered to each other. The lights were so bright, after the darkness, I felt as if the women were shredding my skin."

The image made me shudder. I remembered the sharp glares of the women at the *pa'ndau* exhibit and sale. Had women in Yer's or Millie's family been there?

"Maybe now is a good time to apologize to the ladies," I suggested. "Now everyone is joyful. You could make friends finally. These are our people."

It was unusual for an elder to look a child in the eyes and hold the stare. But Grandma did. Her lip quivered, and her eyes shrank in front of me. Her eyes said she wasn't ready. Maybe there were too many people. I remembered feeling out of place like that, too, on my first day at this school. Maybe she could just meet Yer first at our house, then meet her family later, little by little.

"Okay, let's go home," I said, helping Grandma to her feet.

As we headed for the exit, the boisterous noises in the cafeteria became faint, then silent behind us.

That night my mattress felt like a pile of spent bullet shells. I kept tossing, pelted by all my different emotions. I was still angry, and I wanted to be angry. I had the right to be. Yet at the same time I wanted to embrace my grandmother and bring her along on this adventure, share these wonders with her. But it was as if she had no hands to receive my gifts. Her fingers could curl tightly around a needle, but they would not open. And her eyes, always downcast at her work, wouldn't lift.

Finally, I decided: I'd try a new way to show her, another way to open her hands. Only then did I fall asleep.

The next morning, Saturday, Grandma sent me to the big grocery store. After I bought what we needed, I passed by the extras—the peanut butter was the hardest sacrifice. I used the money to buy special soil and seeds. I chose hot peppers, sweet peppers, cilantro, green beans, and snow peas.

Grandma was in the bathroom when I came home. I

knocked on the door and said, "Come to the back porch when you get out."

In the next few minutes I quickly emptied the soil into window boxes built into the handrails of the landing.

"What are you doing?" Grandma asked when she saw the damp, messy bags.

One at a time I brought the seed packets out from behind my back. Grandma clapped each time she saw the pictures, and I arranged the packets in the boxes. Her smile was almost as wide as the moon, another smile I hadn't seen in so long. A hot pain squeezed behind my eyes.

The first time I'd seen that smile was shortly after I'd finished my first *pa'ndau*. Her son and daughter-in-law, my parents, were stitched in it. On the cloth, baby Mai clung to Grandma's back as we escaped the soldiers and crossed the Mekong River from Laos into Thailand. I'd felt my parents' touch in that *pa'ndau,* and I refused to sell it to traders who offered a lot of money. That's when Grandma had smiled. She must have felt the presence of my parents too.

Now an odd thought trickled from my mind to my heart. If Grandma had brought me to America five years sooner, I never would have learned to embroider so well. I might never have felt the spirits of my parents.

As I helped plant the first seeds, a tear from each eye fell into the soil.

Chapter 15

I met with Miss Susan at the library every morning that summer. We had determined that I would join all my eighth-grade classes in September. That made me nervous, so I worked very hard. Each day Miss Susan pulled a different picture book from the shelf and helped me read it aloud. Then we looked at the globe to find the setting. If the story mentioned food, we looked it up in the dictionary or encyclopedia. Or if a natural disaster was mentioned—a flood, a tornado—I'd learn about that. If the story happened long ago, like one that took place in the Depression, we studied what else was going on then. What were artists painting? What were singers singing? Writers writing? Miss Susan placed the whole world on the table before me, and I never had my fill.

My favorite books were written by a woman like me, a refugee. She set many stories in her homeland, Russia. This artist loved cloth too, and painted pictures of it with the care and attention Grandma gave her reverse appliqué.

"She is very proud of her history," I said. "Look at these painted eggs."

"They are like your *pa'ndau,* Mai," Miss Susan pointed out.

I didn't think much about *pa'ndau* anymore. My eyes were hungry for words!

My favorite story wasn't about fleeing war or coming to a new place. It was about a girl who couldn't read when she was little. Kids made fun of her, and I knew how that felt. Not in Miss Susan's class—not in L.E.P.—but in my other classes. I'd seen only a few Hmong kids raise their hands to answer or ask a question. At the same time I sometimes saw American kids laugh at how the words came out or at a question they thought was stupid. I never raised my hand outside L.E.P. I would rather make believe I didn't understand than raise my hand and lose face.

The first time I read about the girl's teacher in the book, I almost cried. Only he saw what was special about the little girl, and how her mind worked in a different way. How she could make art that spoke more beautifully than the words that described it.

I pointed to the painting of him and said, "Miss Susan, you are this teacher to me."

After a moment she whispered, "That is the nicest thing anyone has ever said to me."

After Miss Susan wiped her eyes, I asked, "You love teaching?"

"I wouldn't *do* it if I didn't love it."

"There are mostly girl teachers," I said. "Are all of them alone, with no children or husband, like you?"

Miss Susan's face turned red and she lowered her chin.

I had offended her! "I'm sorry," I said quickly. "With Hmong, all the girls marry and have babies—like my friend Pa Nhia in Laos. Here in America, too, most Hmong girls don't finish school. So I thought . . ."

Miss Susan patted my hand. "It's okay, Mai. I understand how this can be confusing. Many women who teach have husbands and children too."

"It must be very hard to do all that."

"Yes, it is."

Miss Susan began stacking books and clearing our table. But there was still so much more I wanted to know. I didn't understand how she could not have a husband and still be able to buy food and a house. Grandma could not. Aunt Pa Khu had a husband and a job, but they still could not buy a house.

I dared to ask another question. "Do you get a lot of money to teach?"

Miss Susan laughed out loud. I shouldn't have asked that. It must have sounded so rude.

"I make enough, Mai. Don't worry about me. In fact, I make extra money tutoring you every morning. I received a grant—something like a prize—to try new teaching techniques with immigrants."

Even though I didn't understand everything she had said, it sounded strange. How much money did my tutoring cost, I wondered. Who paid Miss Susan? Why would someone get a prize to teach a Hmong girl?

Then I thought of Yer and Ka Chea and how smart they were. And Dr. Patel, the lady doctor. It seemed American people actually wanted girls to succeed in school and in jobs. I didn't sense that from Uncle Ger, even though he was American in many other ways. And Grandma? Sometimes she seemed proud of my going to school. But I thought she'd be happiest if I stayed home, did pa'ndau, went shopping, and raised vegetables and herbs with her.

I remembered the encouraging words of Miss Sayapong in camp: "Keep learning, Mai. That is how to thank me." Teaching made Miss Sayapong and Miss Susan happy *and* made them money. *Being* taught made me happy. I wished it were possible to be a student forever. If not, maybe I could work in a school. I could be a secretary—a *nice* one.

I wondered how teachers learned to be teachers. I'd have to ask, sometime.

One Saturday morning in the middle of summer, Grandma asked, "You're going out again?" She sat on the couch, up to her elbows in beads and silver trinkets to be sewn onto pa'ndau.

"Yes, to play volleyball." Day and night my friends and I played at Roger Williams Park. "I thought you liked me being with Yer and the other girls."

"I do, but when will you have time to stitch clothes for New Year?"

I shrugged. Grandma swept the frills from her lap and

walked to the calendar on the refrigerator. Every American family had such a calendar. I liked how it made us look like a busy family. And it was only by using a calendar that I had finally taught Grandma the English names for the numbers and the days of the week.

"Dancing is Monday and Wednesday," Grandma said. "Volleyball Tuesday and Thursday. Today is Saturday! So much volleyball is not Hmong."

"It's very Hmong!" I said quickly. "Remember, we played it in the camp?"

"You were a child then. Now you're marrying age. No more games for you. A Hmong husband wouldn't permit it either."

I almost laughed. "Yer and Ka Chea play, and they are marrying age too. . . . I know! Why don't I bring them here to meet you after the game?"

"Both Yer and Ka Chea?"

"Yes—they've even asked why they never see you outside."

Grandma took her place on the couch again, but she didn't begin stitching immediately. Wincing, she rubbed her right shoulder and arm.

"Are you okay?" I asked.

"Oh yes, it's the bed here. It's too soft. I must have slept on it wrong. Anyway, yes, you may bring the girls here. You will be thirsty after playing?"

I nodded and skipped to the door. "We'll be home when both clock hands are on the twelve."

When I asked Yer and Ka Chea to walk me home and meet Grandma, they said, "Sure," like it was nothing at all. I wondered if they'd been shy, like me, when they first arrived. Maybe they were born friendly. Everyone liked them, except for Heather. And whenever we went someplace together, Hmong boys gathered around us like bees around honeysuckle! They didn't climb all over us, like Lue and Lisa did with each other. They just talked and acted silly. I never said anything. What *would* I say to a boy? Sometimes we played on the same volleyball teams—mixed boys and girls—and I was afraid I'd fall into someone. But part of me wanted to show off how good I was. Maybe I got that part from Grandma. I remembered watching her negotiate prices for our *pa'ndau* in camp. She was proud of her skills.

There was one boy, a Hmong boy named Shawn, at the park that day. I knew him from school. He often directed his questions and comments to me. I didn't know why—I never answered him. Yer teased me sometimes, saying, "Shawn likes you. He told me so." I never answered her either. I just turned my face away and ignored them.

After we warmed up at the park, team captains chose sides. Shawn picked me! I felt as if someone had drenched me with cold water—shivery and jumpy. He placed me next to him on the middle line to start. We both played well as we rotated around the court. Then when we were playing deep on the back line, a serve sped to a spot in front of and between us, a place where no one was playing. Shawn and I dived for the ball at the same time. I popped it back up in the air just before Shawn landed on me.

Ugh, it hurt! His elbow had landed right in the middle of my back. I rolled on the ground, not able to reach the hurting part.

"Oh, are you okay? I'm so sorry," he said, helping me up.

The kids gathered around. Yer was giggling, but I wasn't. It really hurt! Maybe I'd broken a rib. Shawn rubbed the spot and led me to a picnic table in the shade. Keeping his hand on my back, he sat with me and asked, "Should we call 911? Or would you prefer a shaman?"

"I'm all right," I fibbed. "You can go back and play."

"No, I think we both should take a break," Shawn said.

His arm never left my back. That surprised me—to do that in public. What if a Hmong adult saw us?

The match continued, and soon Shawn had me laughing as he described it play by play. He had nicknames for everyone. Yer became "Yer the Terror" and Ka Chea became "Catchy Cold."

"And you're 'Showoff Shawn,'" I said.

He faced me, his mouth drooping and his chin dropping.

Oh, no, I had hurt his feelings. "I didn't mean it, it's just that you're so good and—"

He erupted in laughter. "I knew I could get you.

You're still a refugee who will believe anything anyone tells her."

"I can't help what I am," I mumbled, winding my shorts' drawstring around my finger. But he had begun walking away from the courts, away from me. *Raum!* How could I be so mean and stupid? I tried to concentrate on the volleyball so I wouldn't become upset. My team was losing without Shawn and me. Just when I stood to rejoin the game, an orange ice cream on a stick appeared in front of me.

"Peace offering?" Shawn asked with a bold smile.

I couldn't refuse it. Just as I reached for it, he bit off the top half, showing the white ice cream inside. I wanted to punch him!

His mouth still full, he said, "And let me show you how to lick the bottom, too, so it doesn't drip down your hand."

Maybe I should have called him a pig instead of a showoff! Before I could say another word, he pulled a brand-new ice cream from behind his back and gave it to me. I laughed so hard, I forgot about my ribs.

Unwrapping the treat, I said, "This refugee won't ask if you want a taste!"

When the kids stopped playing, we all headed home. Shawn stayed by my side until we reached my block.

"This is far enough, I think, or else my grandmother will scold me," I told him.

"You can just knock her down like you knocked me down playing volleyball," Shawn said.

"Huh? Who's the one who got hurt?"

"Right. . . ." He crossed his arms and cocked his head. "You're pretty tough, huh?"

I shrugged, wondering if he liked tough girls.

"The way you dived for that ball. You didn't care about your hair or your nails or if you got dirty. You just went after what you wanted," he said with a smile. As he jogged away, he called, "From now on I'm calling you 'Mai the Mauler'!"

Up ahead, Yer and Ka Chea taunted me, "Mai is a mauler" and "Mai's mauling Shawn." I would be lying if I said I didn't like it.

As we walked up the front steps, we heard Heather and Lisa yelling in their apartment. Soon Uncle Ger's and Grandma's voices came loudly out the screenless window too. Yer and Ka Chea nudged each other.

"You know," I said, "maybe today isn't such a good day to meet my family. Maybe we can visit after volleyball next Tuesday night?"

My friends nodded quickly and jogged off.

I stopped on the landing outside my cousins' open door and listened to Heather screaming at my uncle. Stunned, I couldn't believe she spoke to adults that way. At the same time, I wished I had the courage to speak up to Grandma like that.

"Stay out of this, Heather," Uncle Ger ordered. "It has already been settled. It's Hmong tradition—something you never cared about!"

"You're right! I don't care if a bridal price is tradition," Heather argued. "We learned in school that you can't sell people like slaves for a few thousand dollars. You don't negotiate for people's lives. No way am *I* marrying into a Hmong family. Lisa can have her Hmong husband."

Oh, no! Someone had told my uncle about Lue and Lisa.

"I don't care what name you call yourself now, you are Hmong," Grandma growled. "Obey your father!"

Heather just sucked her teeth really loud.

Lisa pleaded, "Heather, remember, I *do* want to get married. Be happy for me!"

"You're fifteen! How do you know what you want? And Lisa, Lue doesn't want to get married so young. Not until he finishes high school, remember? The marriage won't even be legal until you're sixteen! And I'm supposed to marry his older brother who dropped out of school to work . . . at a gas station?"

Oi, Heather was to be married too?

"Shh," Aunt Pa Khu pleaded. I saw her shuffling between my cousins and Uncle Ger. Then she stopped. "Mai! You're home!"

Uncle Ger, Aunt Pa Khu, and Grandma pinned me with their eyes. All I could do was twitch, trapped like a mouse.

"Mai, did you know that Lisa and Lue have been together for so long?" Uncle Ger asked. "And that Heather was still seeing this Bobby?"

Heather shook her head and mouthed "no" behind my uncle's back. But I hadn't had her habit of lying for as long as she had. I gazed at Lisa and begged her to see the sympathy in my eyes. "Yes, sir," I answered my uncle.

He shook his finger at me. "I'll deal with you later, Mai, for keeping the truth from me."

I wanted to shout, *Didn't you and Grandma keep the truth from me for five years?* But I was too terrified to speak.

Heather started in again on her father. "You pretend to be American—with your job and your church and your doctors. But when *we* act American, you punish us."

"Your behavior would be a disgrace no matter where we lived!" Uncle Ger yelled, shaking with fury.

"Well, I'm not living *here* anymore!"

"No!" Aunt Pa Khu screamed. "Heather, please, do not be a *laib*."

"Right! It's all a *lie!*" Heather said. She pushed me aside from the door and stepped into the hall.

"Heather, don't!" Lisa cried, held back by Uncle Ger.

Heather flew down the stairs and out the door. I followed her and called, "Where are you going?"

Heather trotted backward, grinning like she'd just won a championship. "I'm going where nobody can buy me or lie to me." Then she spun around and ran down the middle of the street. At the corner she turned left toward Bobby's neighborhood, and she was gone.

Oh, how I missed her already.

I returned to the house, where Lisa was sobbing in Aunt Pa Khu's lap.

"So, it's settled, Lisa," Uncle Ger said, pacing. "If Lue's

negotiators agree to our offer, *you* will be married at least. Thank God we know *his* family is good. I can't say the same of our own."

I felt hollow as dried bamboo. I pictured the future: Lisa would become a wife like Pa Nhia had, and would move into Lue's parents' home, of course. She would leave school to have a child, then a second, then a third, probably more. She and Heather would always be my cousins, but they wouldn't be there for me. I was alone again. Everything had changed, yet nothing really had.

Chapter 16

When we returned to our apartment upstairs, Grandma's hands were shaking and sweat had broken out on her forehead. She fell to the couch and whispered, "Water." When I came back with it, she was dabbing her brow with a *pa'ndau* piece she'd been working on. She drained the glass in one gulp.

Our apartment was completely silent except for my thundering thoughts. Finally, as Heather would have wanted it, I spoke up. "Grandma, why do you approve of Heather and Lisa's marriages, but you didn't want me to marry Yia?"

Panting, she pressed her chest with one hand and placed the glass on the table with the other. "You're smart. They are not," she whispered. Then she closed her eyes and slumped back into the cushions.

I asked the next question easily, naturally, the same way I would snip a thread after I'd knotted it against the cloth. "If I was so smart, why didn't you bring me to America sooner? To the schools, to the healers, five years sooner?"

Grandma's chin dropped and her hand opened. Her *pa'ndau* fell to the floor.

I had finally gotten the words out, and she had fainted! She hadn't even responded, hadn't even tried to explain herself. It was clear she didn't want to talk. But it felt so good to me to be rid of this question, I had to get my answer. I knelt beside the couch and tapped Grandma's hand impatiently. But she didn't stir.

"Grandma." I jostled her arm, but it gave no resistance.

"Grandma!" I said louder. I bent over her, not sure if I was feeling her breaths or mine, her faint heart or mine, now pounding in panic.

"Grandma!" I screamed, standing and backing away. "Grandma!

"Grandma, wake up!

"Grandma!"

What had I done?

In rushed my uncle and aunt. Uncle Ger grabbed Grandma's wrist, then told Aunt Pa Khu to call 911. Shouldn't she call the shaman, too? I thought. After my aunt got off the phone, she wrapped her arms around me. I couldn't stop shaking.

An ambulance crew soon arrived, put a mask over Grandma's face, and strapped her onto a stretcher. Grandma wouldn't have wanted strangers to touch her. She'd want the shaman if it was this serious.

"Where's a shaman?" I asked, my throat tight.

Uncle Ger waved his hand, shooing away my request. "I believe Grandma has had a stroke or a heart attack. The doctors know what to do. I have seen it. Didn't the doctors take good care of you?"

I lowered my eyes in respect. A doctor might be able to fix Grandma's heart, but she needed the shaman, too. Still looking down, I persisted. "Grandma's soul has sunk to the ground."

Uncle Ger rubbed his chin. "Don't argue with me, Mai. I know what's best."

I shivered as the emergency crew wheeled Grandma into the ambulance. Uncle Ger climbed in the back alongside the stretcher, the door shut, and they were off.

"What about her soul?" I cried over the siren.

Aunt Pa Khu squeezed me tighter and said, "We know Grandma has been depressed. It happens to many old ones. But the shaman isn't the only one who can help. American doctors can take care of souls, too. There's even medicine—"

"Grandma won't take American medicine," I muttered.

"Mai, Mai," Aunt Pa Khu said. "Maybe you'll feel better if we pray for Grandma together."

She drew me into their apartment and pressed my hands together like the Thai greeting. We knelt in front of Jesus on a plastic cross, and she said a Christian prayer. It didn't make me feel any better, so I doubted it would help Grandma at all.

Afterward Aunt Pa Khu called a neighbor to give us

a ride to the hospital. Then I helped her gather our immigration papers. She seemed very methodical, like she knew exactly what to do.

By the time we arrived at the hospital, the doctors had Grandma breathing well and awake. But we couldn't see her yet.

"She's being moved to a critical care section," Uncle Ger said. "It's on the fourth floor, and we can wait there more comfortably."

Upstairs, I stared out at the busy Saturday traffic. Leading toward the Hmong neighborhoods in the south were streets named Peace and Friendship. Even though all the women who did *pa'ndau* and all the clan relatives lived here, Grandma had chosen not to stroll the streets of our "village." Instead, she had stayed in the apartment, losing herself in stupid TV shows she didn't even understand.

Or had I gotten her lost? . . . Yet how many times had I offered to read to her, to help her with English, to explain the labels on our American food? Then why did I feel so guilty?

Because I had left her. I hated being needed by her. Hated seeing her needy.

I squatted on the waiting-room floor and sobbed into my crossed arms.

After a long time someone laid a hand on my shoulder. "Grandma's okay," Lisa said. "She wants to see you."

My bout with threadworm hadn't prepared me for this sight. Tubes ran into Grandma's arms and nose like streams to a thirsty river. Machines beeped, pumping out strips of paper. Medical instruments clattered while nurses chatted and giggled behind flimsy white curtains. The air smelled of death, wiped clean.

"Grandma, it's me, Mai. Can you hear me?"

Grandma slowly rolled her head, her eyes fearfully questioning all the tubes and machines.

I winced. "I know. I asked for a shaman, but Uncle Ger . . ." I shrugged. "How do you feel?"

"Tired," Grandma mouthed. "Very tired."

I was feeling so many things at once that I didn't know what to say or do. A part of me was still angry, but I had to keep Grandma calm. She looked pitiful—pale and shriveled like a pepper dried in the sun. It occurred to me that I'd never seen her ill. She had always been—

"Mai, in the camp I was selfish. I was so afraid I would have nothing here. I would not belong here."

She must have heard my question in the apartment after all. And here was her answer. I saw no fireworks, heard no triumphant drums, felt no more freedom than I had a week ago. Maybe peace would come later.

Speechless, I patted her hand.

"And it was true," Grandma whispered. "I don't belong here."

"No, Grandma, you have our family—"

"Not the way it used to be. Here, See is Heather and Pa Cua is Lisa. Here, it is hard to live the Hmong way. And I don't know how . . . to be anything else."

She licked her lips and closed her eyes. I wanted to kiss her, but at that moment the curtain rattled open. Uncle Ger motioned for me to make room for the doctor. I watched the doctor check instruments and listen to Grandma's breathing and heartbeat. In a blink Grandma had fallen asleep. But the doctor didn't seem to care.

"She's doing as well as can be expected," he stated. "Her chances are good. However, her tests from Thailand show that she suffered a mild heart attack some years ago. With medication and exercise, though, she has a good chance of pulling through."

Uncle Ger sighed. He looked first at my aunt and then at me. "You understand? She should be okay."

I nodded, relief spreading through me like warmth from hot tea. Aunt Pa Khu bustled Lisa and me off to the hospital cafeteria, while Uncle Ger stayed with Grandma.

When we returned to Grandma's room, a shaman was setting up his altar on the bedside table. Uncle Ger had decided, after all, that Grandma needed *hu plig* to unite her souls. Grandma's wrinkled skin was the color of elephants, but she was awake and looked content.

I smiled at Uncle Ger, and he shrugged. "The doctor said it was okay, as long as the shaman didn't light any incense or sacrifice any animals. He said the ceremony might actually do Grandma some good."

"Thank you, Uncle," I said.

The shaman's tools and practices fascinated me as

much as the modern medical equipment all around us. I'd never watched a soul calling. I'd been too sick to watch when it was done for me.

His face half hidden in a transparent black veil, the shaman began. He placed the spirit paper money over Grandma, then set up his water bowls, rice bowl, and spirit basket. He gently struck a gong three times to protect Grandma from the haunting *dab:* the ghost demons, eclipse devils, bad footprint spirits, and wild jungle spirits. The shaman lifted his two buffalo horns into the air, then threw them to the floor. One spun, then stood straight up. The other tumbled under the bed.

He pulled back his veil and filled his mouth with water. He sprayed it across Grandma and chanted,

"I will blow the good water for you.
I am strong and not afraid."

Veiled again, he shook, grimacing and grinning in his trance. His rattle jangled to let Grandma's dispersed life souls know he was coming to unite them. There wasn't anything close to a symbolic horse for him to use, so he rode a small step stool into the spirit world. Had he found Grandma's soul? Could he do *hu plig* without the animal sacrifice?

At last the shaman tied strings around Grandma's wrists to bind her souls together. He motioned for each of us to do *khi tes* too. Stooped and sweating heavily, he allowed Uncle Ger to help him pack up. The shaman would come home with us, and we would eat together.

Grandma's eyes shone. Uncle Ger kissed her forehead, and so did I.

"We'll let you rest, Grandma," I said. "You'll feel better tomorrow."

My ears filled with ringing, ringing, bullets pinging against rock, glasses tinkling and toasting to a new life, the shaman clinking his finger cymbals, striking his gong, inviting the *dab vaj* and *dab tsev.*

"Hello? Hello?"

I opened my eyes. Where was I? I wasn't in my bed, my bed of wonderful dreams. I must have fallen asleep at my cousins', I realized. Uncle Ger was standing at my feet, at the foot of the couch. He was holding the phone.

"Who is this?" he asked shakily.

Aunt Pa Khu shuffled toward him, tying her robe. She looked at me, putting a finger to her lips.

Uncle Ger stared at the phone, as if that would help him hear better. Then his face twisted in pain. "I understand," he muttered, his eyes squeezing shut.

Lisa had come out by now. And after Uncle Ger hung up, all he had to do was say my name and I knew what had happened.

I wailed, curling up in a ball. "She can't die. We did *khi tes.* She was getting better. The doctor said so. We prayed to your God, Aunt Pa Khu. Didn't we pray for Grandma? Did I do it wrong?"

My uncle knelt beside me and placed his hand on my arm. "Shh, Mai. The shaman's buffalo horn pointed straight up in the hospital," he said quietly. "I saw it, and knew then—"

"It's the shaman's fault, then! All his fault."

"Shh," Uncle Ger murmured, standing.

I took a deep breath and tried to stop shuddering. Aunt Pa Khu, standing by the dark window, rocked Uncle Ger in her arms. I felt sorry for him, too. He had lost his mother. I knew how that felt.

"We had so much more to say," I moaned.

Lisa sat down and hugged me. "You'll see her again. You'll have her wandering soul for a while. And someday you'll be with her in Heaven—I mean, the Ancestral Kingdom . . . whatever."

Lisa's words didn't help me, and for a moment I was furious at Heather for upsetting Grandma. I had never seen everyone so angry. But what about *my* argument with Grandma?

"*Ntxhais,*" said Uncle Ger, opening his arms to me.

"Daughter," repeated Aunt Pa Khu.

I let them embrace me, but I could not let them comfort me. "I killed her," I sobbed. "I wanted to know why I was left behind five years ago."

"*Ntxhias,* shh," whispered Uncle Ger. His wide hand stroked my head. "You didn't kill her. My mother was old, her heart was weak—the tests showed that. Please, don't blame yourself. You brought her much happiness. More happiness than *we* brought her, I'm ashamed to say."

But Grandma had heard my fiery words. I wanted *her* arms, not Uncle's, around me, reassuring me. As much as I wanted Grandma's soul with me for guidance, I feared it might haunt us all. For Grandma had died without family around her. She had died alone.

Chapter 17

Sleep did not return to me that night. In my cousins' room Lisa snored. I got up and tiptoed toward the lighted kitchen. My aunt and uncle's whispers of funeral plans seeped out from under the swinging door. They discussed Hmong rituals as if they were ordering from a catalog that came in the mail. No, an ox was too expensive to sacrifice. A pig would do. Plus it would make it easier to feed all the guests. No, of course Grandma would not lie in state on a stretcher at home.

"Nobody I know does that anymore," Aunt Pa Khu said. "The smell . . ."

"The funeral parlor is fine," Uncle Ger decided. "I know one that lets Hmong burn incense and paper money there. . . . I also think a soul-releasing ceremony is too un-Christian."

"But your mother, Ger," Aunt Pa Khu said, "was not a Christian."

"She was *my* mother. And I have made up my mind."

I did not recognize the names of the spirit guide and the descendent counselors they discussed. I prayed that

Grandma knew and respected them. The *qeej* player we had already heard at the cultural arts fair. Grandma liked the way he danced. And I thought he was much better than any flute or woodwind player I'd seen on TV.

Aunt Pa Khu sniffled and said, "We must find Heather and tell her."

Uncle Ger's voice grew louder. "You and Lisa can do that. She probably wouldn't talk to me."

I had been the last to see Heather, and she'd been heading toward Bobby's house. I'd tell my aunt in the morning.

Silently, I let myself out and climbed upstairs to our apartment. Grandma would need to be laid out in ceremonial *pa'ndau,* so our ancestors would welcome her and her third soul would be magnificently reincarnated. I tried to imagine her spirit taking a different shape. Would she be punished for lying to me? Maybe she'd become a toad or a monkey. Surely her lie to me wasn't bad enough to send her back as a rock. A rock never dies, so it can never be reborn.

Trudging into my room, I caught my green curtains waving gently with the breeze. How could I have been so selfish about that stupid cloth? I could have made Grandma something. I opened my closet and rooted around for the *pa'ndau* pieces I hadn't sold at the craft fair. I hadn't added to my meager collection in months. I had planned to use my vest for a new Hmong New Year outfit. But now Grandma needed it.

I searched every closet for Grandma's bag of finished

pieces. I opened every drawer, every cupboard. I lifted Grandma's mattress off the floor and found nothing.

Confused, I wandered into the living room, lit only by a three-quarter moon. Grandma's shawl sprawled across the couch. I wrapped it around me and breathed in Grandma's scent of limey fish sauce and garlicky sweat. Even though I didn't remember Grandma ever washing this shawl, it didn't smell bad at all. And Grandma had never taken to using deodorant. "I've smelled the same for seventy-five years," she once said. "Why change now?" I laughed silently, admitting that Americans *were* obsessed with odor.

Oi! Something jabbed my foot. I sat on the couch and pulled out a needle from my heel. I turned on the light and realized I had stepped on the *pa'ndau* Grandma had dropped when she had her heart attack. I glanced around, wondering if her angry spirit had planted that needle just for me. Almost finished, the *pa'ndau* was an appliqué dream maze, the pattern for burial. So Grandma had been preparing for her death— dying slowly, probably since she'd left Asia. I was too blinded by this new, new *everything* to see it. If we had come five years sooner, would she have died five years sooner?

The needle felt cool and smooth between my fingers. It had been over three months since I had done any sewing. My calluses had actually begun to soften. I wondered if I could stitch anymore. If I even wanted to. Wouldn't every stitch feel as if Grandma's fingers were clamping down on mine? I could just hear her: "No, snip there. . . . Closer, stitch closer. . . . No material should show beneath. . . . Mai, your thread is twisted. Mai, mind what you're doing!"

Mind what I'm doing, I thought. Though I knew that no embroidery work should be done during the thirteen-day state of mourning, I plunged Grandma's needle into the cloth and completed her burial collar in about an hour. Then I wrapped it around myself and cried like an infant.

The next morning Aunt Pa Khu was on the phone when I came down. I waited until she was done to speak up.

"Please not now, Mai," she explained. "I have a hundred calls to make about Grandma."

In the kitchen Lisa brought up Heather before I even spoke.

"I just called Bobby's house and got the answering machine," she informed me. "I left a message for Heather."

"Yeah, that's where she seemed to be heading," I mumbled. "Do you think Bobby and Heather would go away together?"

Lisa nodded, chewing on some toast. "Someplace with no Hmong, probably, or word would get back to Daddy. She might go to a town with a lot of Asians, where she could just blend in. Round-eyed whites think we all look the same anyway."

Lisa or I stayed near the phone all morning, but all the calls were for my aunt.

Lisa grew impatient. "Mai, you stay here in case Heather calls. I'm going to get Lue, and we'll go over to Bobby's and get her."

While my uncle trudged through South Providence to make arrangements for Grandma, Aunt Pa Khu and I spent the afternoon working on Grandma's outfit. I did end up sharing the green cloth, as we needed a wrapped skirt for Grandma. Aunt Pa Khu used herself as a model and stitched a few seams.

Lisa came through the door right before dinner. My aunt's eyes flew to her for information. Lisa shook her head and said, "They're gone. We called a bunch of Bobby's friends and relatives, but. . . ." She ended with a small shrug. My aunt disappeared into the bedroom.

At about seven o'clock she reappeared in a plain black dress. "Mai, are you ready for the wake? It may be very difficult."

I nodded. I'd never seen a dead person up close before, none that I remembered. My parents had died when I was three, and we had fled west immediately toward Thailand. I remembered their smiles the way people remember the pictures of loved ones, more than the loved ones themselves. That is quite a trick the mind plays, framing the loved ones silent, motionless, unable to feel pain, but still able to cause it.

Uncle Ger met us at the entrance to the funeral home. It was like a fancy castle. Quietly we walked down a darkly paneled hall past other rooms where dead people lay. Inside the rooms most of the people were seated in rows facing forward, like in a classroom. Many were murmuring and hugging. I actually heard some laughter. I thought nothing could make me laugh again.

My uncle led us into a room the size of our science lab in school, but it looked more like a king's chamber. Thronelike chairs made a U around the room, with rows of regular chairs in the middle. Paneling went halfway up the walls, then green-and-gold fabric reached to the ceiling. The room's curtains fell luxuriously to the floor. Everything was luxurious. Maybe Americans and Christians also believed that the fancier the ceremony and clothes, the sooner the dead person would find peace. When people died in camp, there were drummers and *qeej* players, and the bodies wore *pa'ndau*. Funeral ceremonies spilled out of the huts, with people following the body raised on a stretcher to the camp graveyard. Hiding, I used to watch the friends and family of the dead person, wondering if I would ever have so many people love me.

My aunt and uncle were the first to approach Grandma's casket. They chanted wishes in Hmong, then put their hands together and prayed in English.

I didn't know what to say when I knelt at the casket. So I didn't say anything. Grandma looked serene, not grouchy as she had been these last months. Her casket was mahogany—no nails or clasps, Uncle Ger reassured me. Anything metal would bring ill health to us or to Grandma's souls. The film of tears in my eyes made Grandma waver and sparkle, as if she were already part of the otherworld.

Aunt Pa Khu had done a beautiful job dressing Grandma. She wore hemp slippers with curled toes, so she'd be safe walking through the land of giant furry caterpillars. My vest fit a bit snugly on Grandma, but the patterns of eight-pointed stars, hearts, and diamonds-in-the-squares would bring Grandma luck, love, and protection. During this life she had had little of that.

After Lisa and I visited Grandma, I went to sit on a folding chair in the middle.

"Psst," Lisa said, motioning me over to the wall. "We get to sit in these. The fancy chairs are for the dead person's family."

I found myself chuckling and immediately understood why some mourners in the other rooms were laughing. It felt good, at first, but then I felt guilty for being comfortable when Grandma had had so much pain in her life.

The room soon filled up with many of the people who had first welcomed us to Providence, with coworkers of my aunt and uncle, and with friends of Lisa and Heather. Several times I overheard my aunt fibbing that Heather had just flown out to Fresno, California, and that she couldn't get back in time.

After she chatted with some neighbors, Lisa plopped down next to me and whispered out the side of her mouth. "I hate this part the most. I wish Hmong and Christians would bury bodies right away and get it over with. Dad said that back in Laos they wouldn't bury the body until all the family had arrived. Sometimes that would take ten days! Two more days of this before the burial—ugh!"

I shivered, feeling haunted already. Every time I looked at Grandma, I saw her fingers move. If chickens continued to move after they died, wouldn't people? This thought made me feel ashamed—putting a lowly chicken in the same thought as Grandma. Then it occurred to me that I'd never seen her hands idle before. Perhaps she was now threading herself into our ancestral line. Or maybe, if she was to become an animal, she'd be weaving a new nest.

Lisa elbowed me when Yer and Ka Chea came by.

"We're so sorry," Yer said. Ka Chea's eyes gave me sympathy too. They sat in folding chairs near me. Renée, Millie, and Lag joined us a few minutes later. Their dance had given Grandma such joy. Even though they never did meet, I hoped Grandma saw this show of respect. I felt pride in my friends, and I felt my heart grow stronger, the way a mended cloth holds tighter.

Lisa and Lue stole off while the *qeej* player twirled one-footed and blew his whispery notes. The songs from his bamboo pipes sounded as though they had whistled down from the highlands.

I closed my eyes and pictured Grandma's hard but satisfying life in a Laos that was peaceful. Strapping her babies to her back while farming rice, poppies, and corn on the terraced hillsides. Running after my father and Uncle Ger and other children, now dead and gone too. Threshing and milling rice. Shooing chickens with her feet. Being strong for her husband, but submissive? Not Grandma. I would never forget how she bossed around the pa'ndau traders in the camp. I vowed to picture these scenes every time guilt and shame revisited me.

Four days later, still no word from or about Heather. I couldn't tell if Uncle Ger and Aunt Pa Khu were mourning her, too. Everyone in the house was somber. But today they came out dressed for work.

"But the thirteen days of mourning . . . ?" I asked at breakfast.

Uncle Ger didn't apologize. He simply explained, "We need the money. We cannot afford to miss more work. If it were September, Mai, you'd be returning to school."

I tried Aunt Pa Khu. "Shouldn't we perform the soul-releasing ceremony at least? Grandma's soul could be stuck here on earth forever."

"Don't worry," Aunt Pa Khu said. "God is taking good care of her in Heaven."

I shook my head, not comprehending how this new God worked. He let Grandma die, and now he would take care of her? Aunt Pa Khu said she'd be taking me to their church from then on. She might have to *make* me go, I thought.

After my aunt and uncle left, Lisa crept up beside me. "Bobby called his mother and said he and Heather are fine."

"Where are they?" I blurted.

"Bobby didn't say. But he wants to stop in at home and pick up some things. And he wants me to bring over some clothes and stuff for Heather."

"Then we'll see her?"

Lisa sighed and her shoulders sagged. "No . . . I'm supposed to leave them out on their front porch. He's going to pick them up in the middle of the night—he didn't even say which night." Lisa started to cry.

I put my arm around her and said, "You must miss her ten times more than I miss her."

"She won't even talk to me!" Lisa sobbed. "No offense, but you're just a cousin, and you've only been here nine months. But I'm her sister!"

"All this marriage talk scared her, I bet."

"Heather's never been scared of anything." Lisa dried her eyes. "Well, Mai, let's get you moved into our apartment."

It only took two hours to move my clothes, our food, and a few other items downstairs. What little furniture we had would be left behind. We gave Grandma's clothes back to the church, except for her shawl, her overcoat, and her boots. I planned on growing into them.

I moved into Heather and Lisa's room—well, Lisa's room now, until she got married next month. I just hoped that I wasn't moving into the middle of all their

family fights. Over the foot of my bed I hung my first and favorite storycloth.

"Pretty cool," Lisa said, admiring the *pa'ndau*. "You really are great at this stuff. Look! There are the beer bottles from the camp and that disgusting dried fish. . . . Why doesn't the *pa'ndau* have a border?"

"When I started, all I sewed was borders of Grandma's *pa'ndau*. I guess I got sick of borders." I fingered the frayed edges and quietly added, "I thought I'd never leave."

Lisa pointed to the bloodied forms of my parents stitched on the hut floor. "Oh, man," she whispered. We remained silent awhile. Then Lisa slung her arm around my shoulders. "You've sure had a tough life, Mai. But look at it this way: It can't get any worse."

I really wanted to believe her.

We added a picture of Grandma, and her favorite needle, to the family altar and burned incense in her honor. Someone with a camera had caught her by surprise at the party our first night in Providence. She was laughing.

I didn't remember when Grandma had laughed last. I'd forgotten what it did to her face. Her cheeks puffed up under her eyes, and her top lip stretched above her gums. For someone so old, she certainly had a lot of good teeth left. She didn't care for betel nuts, so her teeth had never turned dark red. I hoped my teeth would last that long. Some old Americans who had false teeth looked like baboons.

Over the next days every thought of Grandma felt like a fist below my ribs. Lisa was off, busy with wedding plans, and soon she'd be really gone. Heather hadn't called or written, but Bobby did pick up their things, Lisa reported. How many times had I seen Uncle Ger pause by the altar and sigh? Aunt Pa Khu had lost so much weight, her skin hung like wrinkled cloth. Grandma hadn't brought me to America to be with a torn family. But what could I possibly do?

At least I had Yer and Ka Chea to keep me from dwelling on my sorrow. We practiced our dances for New Year every other night now. And school would start next week. Eighth graders got computer lab. I couldn't wait!

At the end of September the Yang clan chief married Lisa and Lue in a small private ceremony. It was against the church and state laws to get married so young. Uncle Ger said that they could marry legally when they were sixteen, and that when Lisa and Lue both were eighteen, a priest from St. Michael's would marry them in the church. Lisa beamed the whole day. I didn't see Lue smile once, until halfway through the big feast at his house. He'd been drinking, and his buddies had to hold him up. Lue's big brother didn't seem sad about not marrying Heather. He was flirting with a different girl every time I looked at him. I wouldn't let him come near me.

Lisa found me in the bathroom late in the evening. "I've talked with Heather!" she whispered. "She and Bobby are living in Falmouth, Massachusetts."

I started to shout for joy, but Lisa clamped her hand over my mouth until I calmed down. At last she let me speak. "How is she? When can we see her?"

Lisa's flat voice took away my excitement. "Don't get your hopes up, Mai. Heather said there was no way she was coming home. She also said she wasn't ready to see you and me yet. Whatever that means."

Not ready *yet*. Did that mean that she might be, sometime?

Chapter 18

Our family—Aunt Pa Khu, Uncle Ger, and I—became very busy. Our calendar was filled with blue ink. I made the volleyball team, so I had practice after school. Then I ran home and did my homework. Then I helped prepare dinner. Only after we'd eaten and cleaned up did I have time to work on *pa'ndau*. I could finish only a sash in time for New Year—just a month away! But it would be the prettiest sash there.

Grandma had shown me her favorite design. I made it to honor her. It was fluorescent green with hot-pink satin trim. Inside the pink border I sewed white reverse-appliqué strips of centipedes. Centipedes meant healing or good health. No threadworm would ever come near me again! I also cut and sewed elephant footprints, for lots of money—well, at least a better understanding of it.

Trying on the sash in front of the mirror, I wondered if I would be lucky during the ball toss. Grandma used to boast that Grandfather tossed only with her for the whole five days of New Year back in Laos. She must have been clever and pretty when she was my age. Not as skinny as me, not as shy either. She must have been a lot like . . . yes, Heather.

I had loved to make Grandma tell me about my own parents, and I could still hear her voice in my mind. "Your mother was quite a prize," she said. "Her needle-work was the best in all of Laos. But she had no chance against my son. He sang the sweetest songs to her and made up the cleverest poems. He got his storytelling ability from me, no doubt." Heather was not humble either. I chuckled to picture Grandma at Heather's age. They could have been twins. Both of them would have had flocks of boys flapping around them during the ball toss.

Would Shawn ask me to toss? I would die if I had to sit with the babies during the ball toss. Or worse, with Aunt Pa Khu's friends, who would gossip and scheme up new marriages. Maybe one for me, now that Grandma wasn't around to stop them. But as much as I wanted to toss with a boy my age, I didn't want anyone making marriage plans for me now. I had enough to think about, without having to please someone else.

During one of our telephone conversations, Lisa had told me not to worry so much about the ball toss. "Lots of girls toss with other girls, since many boys are too shy or are playing dumb games outside. It's just a silly old tradition."

Why should she care, anyway? She was married already. "Will you go this year, Lisa?" I asked her. "Your mother and father really need you there—with Heather gone, and Grandma."

"I suppose Lue's parents will take us. But we'll be sitting at their family table, not my father's."

What a quiet and sad table ours would be.

When Aunt Pa Khu came home from the textile factory at six, she admired my sewing. "I'll take you to a good crafts store on Saturday. We'll buy pearl beads and coins to dangle from the sash."

I followed her into the kitchen and set the table. She measured a cup of jasmine rice from a ten-pound bag, and cooked it in the microwave. The humming and beeping box had scared Grandma so much the first time she saw Aunt Pa Khu use it, she hid in the broom closet.

Aunt Pa Khu took out the wok and the vegetables I'd chopped. "Guess who's in charge of mailing all the New Year invitations," she asked me.

"Uncle Ger?" I replied, folding a napkin. "Is that a great honor here?"

"It's a great pain! Over a thousand invitations, a thousand envelopes! A thousand stamps! And guess who is going to help her good aunt and uncle?"

My tongue felt gummy already. "How come so many to mail? Can't we pass some out? Or put up some posters? That's what they do in school."

"Sure, we'll do that to spread the word locally. But Mai, Hmong come to Providence from all over the Northeast—New York, Pennsylvania, and all of New England."

That meant Massachusetts, too. That's how I got the idea.

I couldn't believe how quickly New Year arrived. I strung the last of my beads and coins onto the sash and tied it on over a black flowery dress that Lisa had left behind. I pictured my mother wearing something like it. Jingling and giggling, I twisted in front of the mirror.

"You like it, Grandma?" I called into the air. "Not as well made as yours, of course."

"You're beautiful!" answered Aunt Pa Khu from the doorway.

I felt my face flush, and I quickly told Aunt Pa Khu how lovely she looked. Then Uncle Ger stepped in, handsome in his black slacks and brightly embroidered vest. He pulled something from behind his back. A pile of pa'ndau!

"Grandma's work?" I whispered.

I reached for the intricate stitching, but I couldn't touch it somehow. It was as if my mind could no longer tell my hands what to do.

"Where *were* these?" I asked, my voice scratchy. "When Grandma died, I looked all over for them. I wanted her to wear them for the funeral."

Uncle Ger stuttered a bit. "I apologize. Several weeks before she died, your grandma asked me to keep them for your first New Year in America. She must have known she didn't have much time left." He paused a moment, then added, "She—and I—kept . . . other things from you too."

My chin trembled and I shook my head. My fingers rushed to my lips to stop myself—or him?—from speaking further. I didn't want to hear more words of regret. They were thorns that had pricked enough already.

Uncle Ger cleared his throat. "Well, I apologize. For Grandma, too. As your father, I ask you, please, please wear these."

I gently lifted the top circular piece, a hat. Oh! Cross-stitched centipedes crawling around it—just like my sash. Had Grandma's wandering soul guided my hands? My fingers combed through the cool silver French coins dangling from it. Not the tin imitation coins that were all I could afford for my belt.

"Your grandma brought these francs all the way from Laos," Uncle Ger said. "I remember holding them as a child, so smooth and heavy in my hand."

I put the hat on, and in the mirror it gleamed like a jeweled lampshade. Next I unfolded a three-inch-wide collar. I had studied Grandma's *pa'ndau* technique for seven years, but I had not yet mastered such tiny, delicate stitches. They swirled the finely cut cloth into snail shells, the symbol of family history.

My littlest finger began tracing a shell from the middle—from the center of my Yang ancestry. Slowly I traced the whorls of Yang men who had fought for freedom from the Chinese, Yang women who tried to save the forbidden Hmong alphabet by stitching the characters into *pa'ndau,* Yang who fought the Japanese and then the Communists.

Reaching the outer swirls, I closed my watery eyes. "Grandma . . . Uncle . . . Father . . . Mother," I whispered. I kissed the cloth, pierced by Grandma's sharp needles, clutched by Grandma's knobby hands, examined by Grandma's learned eyes, Grandma's loving eyes. I felt her in every fiber. *There,* she said. *Now we have nothing more to forgive.*

I dabbed my tears with the back of the collar, then draped it around my neck like a scarf. It was so long, I had to tuck it into my sash.

Aunt Pa Khu sniffled. "There's one last thing."

"Oh!" I bowed my head and let her fasten Grandma's silver necklace around my neck. The eight pounds of silver trinkets and charms yanked me downward a little and made me laugh. I adjusted my dress and collar so the necklace wouldn't cut into my skin.

"We must hurry!" Aunt Pa Khu said, bustling after Uncle Ger toward the front door.

Just then the phone rang. I yelled, "I'll get it. It's probably about New Year."

"Mai, it's me," Heather said.

I lost my breath a moment, and almost lost my words. "Heather? Oh, Heather, it's so good to hear your voice. Are you okay? Are you here in Providence for New Year?"

"Mai, cool your jets. I just wanted to thank you for the invitation. Me and Bobby thought that was really nice of you."

"You're coming today, right?" I begged.

"Well, that's another reason I wanted to call," Heather said. "We're not coming. I'm not ready."

It felt as if all the weight of my necklace was pressing on my heart. Was this what Grandma's attack had felt like?

"Mai! Say something," Heather said.

I cleared my throat, but no words came to me.

"Mai, Bobby and I really appreciate what you're trying to do. But if I came home now, my father would win."

"This isn't a game," I whispered, twirling the ends of my sash around my finger.

"I know. I mean, I want him to really miss *me*. Not some dutiful Hmong daughter named 'See,' who I can never be for him."

I nodded. "Maybe New Year next year?"

"Who knows?" Heather said. "Maybe sooner. Have a good time today, and here, someone wants to say hi."

"Hey," said Bobby.

"Hey," I said, with a small grin. "You take good care of my cousin."

"I always have, Mai."

Outside, my aunt and uncle were halfway down the block already. I had to run to catch up, but my heart lightened with every step.

At St. Michael's hall, Hmong of all ages were spilling out of double-parked minivans. All the different license plates! Men carried huge covered pans of food. I longed to peek under the foil—the smells overwhelmed me. Wives bustled in, with babies strapped to their backs. Toddlers tugged at their mothers' pleated skirts. Even the teens had forgotten their "So what?" faces. Ka Chea and Yer waved and met me on the sidewalk.

"Did you make all of these?" Ka Chea asked, touching each *pa'ndau* piece as if she were touching the cheek of an infant.

"Some of them," I said proudly.

"You know, my grandmother's gone now too," Ka Chea said. "Could you teach me to do *pa'ndau?*"

Yer chimed in. "Me, too!"

I felt a burst of heat in my chest. "Yes! Of course!"

"So, are you ready to dance?" Yer said.

With all the emotion of the morning, I'd forgotten about performing in front of everyone. But, strangely, I didn't feel nervous anymore. I'd practiced all summer with my friends, and these were my people, and I just felt purely happy. "I can't wait!" I replied.

"That's the attitude," Ka Chea said.

Someone jingled the coins on my sash. "Wow, you look great!" It was Shawn, in an embroidered vest with rows and rows of silver francs. His hat had stripes of jade and black. *He* looked great! He raised a can of tennis balls and asked, "Will you toss with me, Mai?"

I tried to keep my lips together so he couldn't see how happy I was. But I failed. "It's just a game," I warned him. "Nothing more."

"Oh, you're so tough!" he said, laughing.

Inside the hall, the jingling of belts and hats, combined with the chatter and squeals of children, was so loud, I almost fell backward! Families lined rows of long tables. At one end a stage held microphones, guitars, and drums beneath a huge banner: *Nyo Zoo Xyoo Tshaib!* Happy New Year! A dance space was filling with teens opening cans of tennis balls for the ball toss. Alongside the dance floor important men had already gathered at the table of honor. At the other end of the hall women organized steaming pans of rice, vegetables, and meat.

Suddenly, Lisa appeared at my side and hollered, "Wild, huh?"

I yelled, "I thought you outgrew all this Hmong stuff."

Lisa shrugged and yelled back, "I guess I grew back into it."

"Attention!" called a man over the microphone. "Welcome to the Hmong New Year in Providence!" The hall erupted in shouts, cheers, and applause. The man introduced a woman named You Pao Yang, probably a cousin, somehow. She sang the traditional welcome song:

> "Goodbye, Old Year!
> Take evil, sickness, and death away
> to the end of the horizon
> so we may never see or hear them again."

Pride filled me, and I wanted so badly for Grandma to feel it too. If only we had arrived in America in time for last year's New Year, Grandma would have felt we belonged. She would have seen that we could live here without giving up everything Hmong.

I ran my fingers over my snail-shell collar and whispered, "I'll celebrate for both of us, Grandma." I pictured my parents, and Pa Nhia on the other side of the world, and I pictured Heather and Bobby together building their own new life, and I added, "I'll celebrate for all of us."

I leaned over to look at my aunt and uncle on the other side of the table. Their eyes kept going to the door, hoping for the impossible. I was glad I hadn't told them about inviting Heather. They would have gotten their hopes up too high, and their day would have been ruined from the start. I wouldn't hold back the news for long, though. I knew too well what that empty waiting felt like. I'd tell them tomorrow.

For now I walked over between them and took their hands.

"In camp," I said, "Grandma used to tell me, 'Be patient. Our time will come.'"

They squeezed my hands and focused on the song.

"Welcome, New Year!
We honor you with happiness,
peace, and health.
We hope you bring prosperity forever!"

When the chanting ended, cheers filled the hall. Beaming, Lisa bounded over, arms wide.

"Careful, careful, not so tight," she told her parents as they hugged her. "I think I have a baby in there!"

Everyone's eyes grew wide as shining coins. Mine

did too, as I realized how happy Lisa was about it, not like Pa Nhia.

Voices erupted. "A baby!" And Lue was soon dragged over for handshakes and hugs. I'd never seen so much hugging in my life!

To make room, I backed up a bit—right into Shawn. He was juggling three balls. I snatched one out of the air and said, "Let's go!"

I skipped to the girls' line, which had formed on the dance floor across from the boys' line.

"Oooh, Mai and Shawn," Yer sang out. She and Ka Chea were leaning against the stage. But not for long. Those bees were soon swarming my honeysuckle friends.

As I faced Shawn and began the toss, who did I see right next to him? Yia! Of course—he'd moved to Springfield, Massachusetts. And Koufing—how tall he'd grown in just a year. He was following the arc of his father's toss, prancing between him and a pregnant woman.

Yia waved at me and said, "Mai, this is my wife, Chee! And Chee, this is the girl from Phanat Nikhom I told you about."

A part of me felt silly. What girlish thoughts I'd had about Yia! Of course he would marry as soon as he could. Koufing needed a mother. And Yia needed joy again.

"Is your grandmother here, Mai?" Yia called over.

I almost dropped my ball at the question. Suddenly, I

couldn't find words. My hands touched my sash and my collar, and I thought, *Grandma is here,* and I touched my silver necklace, *here,* and my jingling hat, *here.* Then I lifted my hands high into the air and twirled once slowly, *here and everywhere.*

Yia nodded, with a smile neither joyous nor sad.

"Oi!" The tennis ball hit my hat and knocked it askew.

"Sorry!" Shawn laughed, not looking sorry at all.

Giddy, I whipped the ball at him. He dropped it and had to chase it under a table.

"Now you owe me a song or a poem!" I reminded him when he returned.

"Uh, uh, uh, okay," he said.

> "Mai is beautiful
>   as an orchid,
>   but has the strength
>   of a tiger.

"How's that? Okay?" he asked, tossing me the ball gently.

"I suppose," I said. But surprised at the tiger bit, I whipped the ball again.

"Hey! Take it easy!" he called, barely catching it.

"I thought you liked girls who were tough!" I joked.

We tossed gently for a while, but I vowed to test him again and again. I wasn't ready to be courted any time soon. Unlike Lisa and Heather, I had a lot of school ahead of me.

As all the balls arced back and forth, I caught bright signs of eight-pointed stars, centipedes, shells of the snail. A new year of luck, health, and happiness jingled in the air, and here I was, safe and swirling, inside it.

AFTERWORD

In 1989 my husband, Tom, and I took a trip that changed our lives. We visited Thailand and the Ban Vinai refugee camp, where our dear friend Susan Clements Beam worked. One of about ten such camps housing refugees from wars in Vietnam, Laos, Cambodia, and Myanmar, Ban Vinai served more than 40,000 Hmong and other hill tribe people in a space about as small as a high school campus. Some refugees had spent more than ten years there already.

The Hmong are fiercely independent hill tribes who have populated the southwestern Chinese provinces of Yunnan, Guizhou, and Kwangsi for more than 4,200 years. Estimates of the Hmong (or Miao) ethnic minorities remaining in China are between 5 and 7 million people today. However, in the eighteenth and nineteenth centuries hundreds of thousands of Hmong fled Chinese persecution. They resettled in the remote northern mountains of Vietnam, Laos, Thailand, and Burma (now Myanmar)—the area Western colonizers called Indochina.

Many of these relocated Hmong fought alongside French colonial soldiers against the Japanese, who occupied Vietnam and Laos during World War II. In the early 1950s the Hmong continued to side with the

French, who tried in vain to maintain control of In-dochinese colonies and their lucrative markets.

The controversial involvement of many—not all—Lao Hmong in the Vietnam War was what caused their mass emigration from Southeast Asia. In the 1960s and 1970s the American government secretly employed about 100,000 Hmong men and boys in Laos to sabo-tage the Ho Chi Minh Trail, a system of jungle roads used by the North Vietnamese to supply their soldiers in the south. The U.S. also used Hmong to repair and fly airplanes for bombing missions in North Vietnam, and to rescue downed pilots in the dense, mountainous jungles. When the war ended in 1975, the Americans left the Hmong behind to pay bitterly for opposing the Communist forces. The Pathet Lao, the new Commu-nist rulers of Laos, bombed and gassed Hmong villages, raping and murdering Hmong women and children. Again the Hmong fled, this time across the Mekong River to Thailand.

Numerous refugee camps set up in Thailand housed tens of thousands of Hmong and Lao refugees until 1996—two decades after the war had ended for Ameri-cans! The Thai were also absorbing thousands of refugees from Cambodia in the southeast and from Myanmar in the northwest. The government could not let all these people take over land that belonged to Thai citizens, so the camps held refugees until international agencies could find places for them to live.

This novel takes place around 1994, when the last of

the refugee camps were closing. Meanwhile, U.S. anti-immigrant sentiment escalated and caused problems for incoming refugees. A recent report from the Hmong National Development Organization estimates that more than 250,000 Hmong now live in the United States, in cities, including St. Paul–Minneapolis, Minnesota; Fresno, California; Detroit, Michigan; Milwaukee, Wisconsin; Greensboro, North Carolina; Providence, Rhode Island; and in smaller towns across the country. Other refugees have settled in France, Canada, Guyana, and Australia. Some Hmong have chosen to return to Laos; some have been repatriated to Laos against their will.

In 1997 Hmong who fought alongside Americans won long-overdue Congressional recognition, a national monument, and citizenship-requirement relief.

Pa'ndau, the ancient textile art Mai and Grandma create, is revered in the Hmong culture. *Pa'ndau* adorns dress for the most joyful and most solemn occasions—from weddings, births, and New Year to funerals. While techniques such as batik, appliqué, reverse appliqué, and cross-stitch have been used for millennia, *narrative* storycloths such as those featured in the picture books *Dia's Story Cloth; Nine-in-One, Grr! Grr!;* and *The Whispering Cloth* were first created in the 1960s. Unfortunately, most Hmong girls and women, needing to make a living in America, no longer have time for this stunning stitchwork. The market for the work is small and doesn't bring in much money. The *pa'ndau* art form faces extinction.

GLOSSARY

Hmong Words

Under centuries of persecution in China, the Hmong lost their original written alphabet. A new one, "Pahwah Hmong," reproducing the exact sounds of spoken Hmong, was developed late in the 1950s. Pahwah has its own characters, but Hmong today use the Roman alphabet. Hmong has thirteen vowels and fifty-six consonants.

Hmong is a tonal language—that is, the syllables have higher or lower pitch—with eight tones. The last letter of each word specifies the tone, and is rarely pronounced. A "b" gives the highest tone; a "g" gives the lowest. If a vowel ends a word, there is no tone at all.

dab (dah): Spirits. Most of the good spirits are *dab vaj* (dah va), spirits around the house, and *dab tsev* (dah jay), spirits inside the home. When said without an adjective, *dab* means a bad spirit.

Hmong (mung): The words *Hmong* and *pa'ndau* have become so commonly used by Westerners that they now have English spellings. The Hmong spell their name Hmoob and it means "Free People." Hmong existed as early as 2000 B.C. in mountainous Southwest China.

hu plig (hu **plee**): The Hmong soul-calling ceremony, performed by a shaman (healer) when a person is ill.

khi tes (kee **they**): The strings tied around an ill person's wrist by a shaman to bind the body's wayward souls. This is done during a *hu plig*.

laib (ly): "Gangsta," someone who disobeys parents, skips school, etc.

maum (mom): Endearment meaning little daughter or little girl.

naiban (**ny** bahn): This Laotian term for village leader was used by Hmong and authorities in the refugee camps. Traditionally, the Hmong used *tswv zos* (choo zhow).

niam (nyeh): Mother.

ntsej muag (jay mwa): Literally, "you face," an insult similar to, or even worse than, "you jerk."

ntxhais (ty): Formal word for daughter.

Nyo Zoo Xyoo Tshaib (nya zhuh shuong **chee a**): Happy New Year.

pa'ndau (pah **ndow**): *Paj ntaub* is the official spelling. (See "Hmong" above for explanation.) Flower cloth. The needle-and-thread art form is used today to create wall hangings, ornaments, clothing, and narrative storycloths. Techniques include reverse appliqué,

appliqué, and embroidery styles including cross-stitch and chain stitch.

Pathet Lao (Pah tet low [rhymes with "now"]): Formed in late 1946, this group sided with Communist Northern Vietnam in the frequent warring that followed. In 1975, it overthrew the royal Laotian government to create the Lao People's Democratic Republic. One of its first military objectives was to "wipe out" the Hmong, who had sided with American forces during the Vietnam War.

qeej (keng): A wind instrument with long curved bamboo pipes. Players slowly whirl in circles while blowing.

quav (ko **wah**): Feces.

raum (too uh): Stupid.

Saub (sho uh): The supreme being. Folktales feature Saub as a wise man who can see the future.

tsov tom (jaw taw): Warning. Literally, "tiger bite." Its meaning is "Tiger's going to bite you!" and it is often issued by an elder to a child.

txais tos (sy taw): Welcome.

zis (gee): Urine.

Hmong Names

As in any language, names can be pronounced differently according to preference, tradition, or geographic region. For people who don't speak Hmong, the names are easier to pronounce than the vocabulary words, because the tone rules do not apply. For instance, the "g" in Yang and the "r" in Yer are pronounced just as they would be in English. However, the Hmong clan name is usually said first, followed by the given name. Hmong switch that order when dealing with Americans, and many Hmong now use American names themselves. Here is a pronunciation guide to clan names and given names in this book:

Clan names

Lor (Lor)
Vang (Vang)
Yang (Yang)
Xiong (Song)

Given names

Bee (Bee)
Chee (Chee)
Cher (Cher [sounds like "chair"])
Ger (Jer)
Kah Chea (Ka chee a)

Koufing (Koo fing)
Lag (Lah)
Lue (Loo)
Mai (My or May)
Pa Cua (Pah chew ah)
Pa Khu (Pah koo)
Pa Nhia (Pah nee ah)
Pao (Pow)
See (See)
Yer (Yer)
Yia (Yee ah)
You Pao (Yoo pow)

Thai Words

Thailand still uses its original and ornate alphabet. Here, it is transliterated into Roman letters, as used in this book:

alloy mahk (a **loy** mock): Very delicious.

baht (bot): Thai money, used in the refugee camps. In the early 1990s, one *baht* equaled four American cents. Thai numbers in this story: *sip* = 10; *ha* = 5; *baat* = 8.

kop kum ka (**kop** koom **ka**): Thank you, as spoken by a woman. *"Ka"* is replaced by *"kop"* when spoken by a man.

Meo (**mee** o): This is the name of a real tribe in the northern mountains of Southeast Asia. However, to the

Hmong it has become an insult meaning a barbarian, or an ignorant person.

nitnoy (**nit** noy): A little.

paang mahk (pang mock): Too expensive.

sawat di kop (sa wa dee **kop**): Hello, spoken by a man. *"Kop"* is replaced by *"ka"* when spoken by a woman.

tao ri (tow [rhymes with "now"] **ry**): How much?

tuk tuk (took took): A small taxi or carriage towed by a motor bike.

whai (wy): The action of pressing hands together and bowing head to show respect. The higher one holds the hands and the deeper the bow, the more the respect paid.

Hmong Symbols Used in This Book

Like any culture, Hmong has traditional symbols. Hmong women pass these on through *pa'ndau*. Here are a few symbols that appear in this novel, and their meanings.

Centipedes: Healing and good health.

Cucumber seeds: Seeds, plants, and flowers appear in *pa'ndau* in several ways: In storycloths, they represent the crops farmed and the flowers growing nearby; in both storycloths and traditional patterned *pa'ndau*, they can decorate and fill space; and seeds in patterns can represent abundance.

Diamond-in-the-square: The imprint of the most powerful good spirit; the shape of the home altar.

Elephant footprints: Wealth and power.

Dream maze: This pattern of right angles is used more on burial clothing than as a symbol. The pattern was revealed in a dream to a woman who awoke and immediately stitched it.

Eight-pointed star: Means luck and protection from evil spirits.

Triangles: Pointing down, they can mean sharp teeth, signifying pain; pointing up, they symbolize the mountains of the Hmong homeland; when connected, they symbolize a barrier.

FOR FURTHER READING
ABOUT THE HMONG

Picture Books

Cha, Dia. *Dia's Story Cloth*. Stitched by Chue and Nhia Thao Cha. New York: Lee & Low Books, 1996.

Coburn, Jewell Rice, adaptor, with Tzexa Cherta Lee. *Jouanah: A Hmong Cinderella*. Illustrated by Anne Sibley O'Brien. Arcadia, Calif.: Shen's Books, 1996.

Shea, Pegi Deitz. *The Whispering Cloth: A Refugee's Story*. Illustrated by Anita Riggio, stitched by You Yang. Honesdale, Pa.: Caroline House, Boyds Mills Press, 1995.

Thao, Cher. *Only a Toad*. Green Bay, Wis.: Project Chong, 1993.

Xiong, Blia, with Cathy Spagnoli. *Nine-in-One, Grr! Grr!: A Folktale from the Hmong People of Laos*. Illustrated by Nancy Holm. San Francisco: Children's Book Press, 1989.

Middle-Grade Nonfiction and Folktales

Goldfarb, Mace. *Fighters, Refugees, Immigrants: A Story of the Hmong*. Minneapolis, Minn.: Carolrhoda Books, 1982.

Johnson, Charles, ed. *Myths, Legends, and Folk Tales from the Hmong of Laos,* as told by Pa Chou Yang et al.; written and translated by Se Yang. St. Paul, Minn.: Macalester College, 1985.

Lewis, Paul, and Elaine Lewis. *Peoples of the Golden Triangle: Six Tribes in Thailand.* London and New York: Thames and Hudson, 1984.

Livo, Norma J., and Dia Cha, eds. *Folk Stories of the Hmong: Peoples of Laos, Thailand, and Vietnam.* Englewood, Colo.: Libraries Unlimited, 1991.

Young Adult and Adult Literature

Chan, Anthony. *Hmong Textile Designs.* Owings Mills, Md.: Stemmer House, 1990.

Chan, Sucheng, ed. *Hmong Means Free: Life in Laos and America.* Philadelphia: Temple University Press, 1994.

Faderman, Lillian, with Ghia Xhiong. *I Begin My Life All Over: The Hmong and the American Immigrant Experience.* Boston: Beacon Press, 1998.

Fadiman, Anne. *The Spirit Catches You and You Fall Down: A Hmong Child, Her American Doctors, and the Collision of Two Cultures.* New York: Farrar, Straus, and Giroux, 1997.

Hamilton-Merritt, Jane. *Tragic Mountains: The Hmong, the Americans, and the Secret Wars for Laos, 1942–1992.* Bloomington, Ind.: Indiana University Press, 1993.

Pfaff, Tim. *Hmong in America: Journey from a Secret War.*
Eau Claire, Wis.: Chippewa Valley Museum, 1995.

On the Web

Visit www.hmongnet.org or enter "Hmong" into a search engine for a wide selection of articles about the customs, music, stories, authors, and political issues of Mai's people.

ACKNOWLEDGMENTS

I could not have written this book without the support and interest of many Hmong who opened their doors and hearts to me. First, a special thanks to Mai Neng Moua, a fellow writer, who gave me frank and valuable feedback in the early versions of the novel. Thanks to my friends Shawn Moua and family; Pao and Chee Lor and their boys, Josh, Yancey, Sawyer, and Austin; Yeng and Mao Yang and family; Yia and Mao Lee and family; Sy and Mao Lee and family; Khoua Lee and her boys, Sie and Nusol; You Yang; Chou and Ying Ly and family. My gratitude also goes to Toua Kue, who worked for Catholic Relief Services in Providence, and to Lt. Col. Wangyee Vang, president of Lao Veterans of America. I especially thank my focus group of young Hmong women, who read and discussed the manuscript with me: Pa Nhia Ly, Pa Khu Ly, Ka Chea Natalie Ly, Cua Xiong, Maishoua Ojeda, and May Yang Hanlon.

Many educators helped me get the school scenes right. Topping the list is Erin Connole, a teacher at the Sackett Street Elementary School in Providence, who toured me around the Hmong neighborhood and allowed me valuable access to her classes full of Hmong children. My E.S.L. consultants were Louis Barboza from Roger Williams Middle School, Providence, and Mary Jo

Myslinksi, Margaret Youmatz, Miriam Underwood, and Pamela Callihan, teachers in the Vernon school district, who enlightened me about basic E.S.L. instruction and about the specific needs of local Hmong children. Thank you all for your time and expertise.

I would like to thank the following scholars and refugee activists who provided assistance and direction: Norma J. Livo, who with Dia Cha edited *Folk Stories of the Hmong*; Jane Hamilton-Merritt, author of *Tragic Mountains* and an activist on behalf of the Hmong; Dr. Mace Goldfarb, author of *Fighters, Refugees, Immigrants,* who worked in Ban Vinai, Thailand, and now practices in St.Paul–Minneapolis; Tim Pfaff, author of *Hmong in America* and curator of Public Programs at the Chippewa Valley Museum, Wisconsin; Anne Fadiman, author of *The Spirit Catches You and You Fall Down*, a book about the clash of third-world cultures and medicinal rituals with America's high-tech medicine community; Sumonnat Puttavon, a teaching supervisor in Phanat Nikhom, Thailand; and Greg Hope of Episcopal Migration Ministries. I also thank the Refugee Studies Center at the University of Minnesota for its excellent resources and accessibility.

It feels as though every editor has seen this manuscript in at least one incarnation since 1995. I deeply appreciated all the constructive feedback and thoughtfulness in rejection. In particular, I thank Karen Klockner for urging me to write the novel and for cheering my first efforts; and Dinah Stevenson, who believed that I could make it "better and better." I thank agents Jennifer Flannery and Dwyer & O'Grady for their support in the past. And thank you to Jim Tyrell of D&D Printing for his generosity and patience.

Gratitude and love to my trusted friends and constructive critics of the Wednesday Writers Group: Susan Bivin Aller, Barbara Barrett, Janet Finney, Clavin Fisher, Joan Horton, Janet Lawler, Edna Ledgard, Anita Riggio, Marcia Sanderson, Joyce Sidman, Joyce Stengel, Edith Tarbescu, Nancy Wadhams, Laura Williams; and to Jackie French Koller, a founding member of our group and a role model to me. Thanks also to Gail Gauthier, Moira Fain, and Michelle Palmer for their input. A special lifelong hug to Sue Beam. She started this whole thing in 1989 in complacent Connecticut by showing us pictures of Ban Vinai, where she worked, then giving us our first *pa'ndau*. May you continue to alter lives.

Last but not least, a big slobbery thank-you to my family for believing in me and the book for the past eight years: Tom, Deirdre, and Tommy Shea; George and Peggy Deitz; and the spirit of Nana, who's always with me.